By the same author

The Falling Awake Mysteries:

The Invisible Body

The Long Lost Sunset

The Never Ending Fall

THE NEVER ENDING FALL

Jenny Cutts

STOPPED CLOCK PRESS

STOPPED CLOCK PRESS

First published in 2022 by Stopped Clock Press
Copyright © Jenny Cutts 2022

ISBN 978-1-914001-09-3
Stopped Clock Press Ltd.
Company Number 12829670

www.jennycutts.com

THE NEVER ENDING FALL

I fall awake in my guest room on the top floor. The city sounds have all been sucked away. I get out of bed and stand by the window, the coolness of the glazing inches from my face.

My window overlooks the back of the property: the margin of terrace, the unkempt grass, the neighbouring buildings that ring the space. Silvery moonlight tumbles from the sky, lingering on the sea of scattering grasses.

I look to the ground. It seems a long way down. I watch as a figure emerges: Zoya is dream-walking too.

She paces across the terrace, weaving between the tables and chairs. Then she rolls down the small steep slope that drops away from the paving and comes to rest in the springy, wild growth below: not by accident, but for fun.

I leave my room and make for the stairs.

By the time I walk through the terrace door into the soft night, I see that Zoya is wading around in the meadow. In the soundlessness of the dreaming, I can hear, strangely magnified, the push of her footsteps tearing through the foliage and ruffling the plain of shimmering grass.

Then she sits down, leans back on her elbows and looks at the sky. I hurry – casually – toward her.

'Seen any new constellations?' I ask.

Zoya turns toward me and smiles.

'Do you mind if I join you?' I ask.

'Of course I don't mind.'

I sit on the ground next to her. The night, like all nights in the dreaming, feels tranquil and the surrounding buildings seem to buffer us from the cold, empty loneliness of the deserted city beyond. Above us, stars are revealing themselves, piercing through the city's ambient street-lit haze. The moonlight is strong, bathing us in a magical silver-trimmed light. I can see her clearly. She's looking up at the sky.

'You wouldn't know we were in a city out here,' I say.

'I know. It's nice.'

'Just us and the stars.'

Zoya laughs. 'And all the windows.'

'Well, windows with nobody to look through them,' I say.

She turns to me. 'There *could* be.'

Her voice has a slightly defiant edge. I stand up and cup my hands to my mouth.

'Hello! Is anybody there?'

Not surprisingly, there is no answer to my call.

'There isn't,' I say conclusively.

Zoya laughs again. 'Is that your method?'

She holds her arms out for me to help her to her feet. I pull her up.

'You drive about in your van, wake up in the dreaming, and shout?' she says.

We begin strolling aimlessly through the waves of grass.

'Pretty much.'

'But that's not how you found me. I don't remember any shouting.'

'No…'

'You were climbing up my house, if I recall… and then you ran away.'

We laugh.

'*Alright.*' I feel embarrassed. 'I was just surprised, that's all.' I wonder if she can see the flush of my cheeks in the moonlight.

'I know.'

'Well,' I say, 'about that, I don't think I ever said. That night… I did actually feel drawn to your house.'

'Did you?'

'Yeah. I really did. Because *you* were there.'

'It wasn't the fact that it's the craziest house in Shilly? On top of a hill–'

'… Big whale sculpture on the roof… No. Only a little bit. I felt drawn to go there that night.'

She narrows one eye slightly. 'You didn't.'

'I did!'

'How do you know you're not retrofitting your theory onto it?'

'My theory?'

'Yes. You think we share our dreams, or whatever it is, because… you and I are… a special match.'

I stop walking but she keeps pacing through the garden. 'Don't you think this is special?'

'Yes, of course.' She pauses and turns to face me. 'Of course I think it's special. And I've loved doing *all this* with you.'

'But… you think there might be others.'

'There might be!'

'There aren't.'

'What happened to keeping an open mind?'

She turns to continue her stroll. I catch hold of her hand. 'Zoya.' She turns and I take her other hand as well. 'The thing is, though, that *you're* the only one I *want* to be here… with me.'

She is looking up at me, her dark eyes shining in the moonlight. Will she let me kiss her? We draw closer and kiss softly. I've missed her lips against mine.

And then we are pacing through the garden again and I have kept hold of her hand. After a minute, I ask the question. 'What did I do wrong?'

'Nothing. I just wanted some time on my own.'

'No, really, you can tell me.'

'I just told you.' Then, she flails her arms in exasperation, breaking our touch. 'And I told you in Dublin too!'

I stop walking and put my hands on my hips. 'So, you came all this way, rocked up in Edinburgh, found out where I am, just to stay in the room across the hall?'

'Why are you taking it personally? I did think it would be nice to see you and…'

'Nice?'

'And there's this… idea I want to explore.'

'Your ridiculous idea about Fintan?'

'It's *not* ridiculous.'

'It kind of *is* – because, for one thing, how will you ever know if he was a dreamer, like us? He's dead now so *he* can't tell us. We can't bump into him on a night like this.'

'He might have told someone about it – just because *you* never would!'

'Well, *have* you told anyone yet? What about your dad? What would that be like if you told him that you have this whole other dream life when you're asleep? Don't you think he'll start looking at you like you're crazy?'

She folds her arms. 'You're starting to sound like a controlling boyfriend.' She starts walking back to the house.

'No... I... I'm just trying to stop you getting hurt. Come back... where are you going?'

By now she has reached the terrace.

'Out! Into the city. You know, there's a whole, big, beautiful city out there?'

'Zoya! Don't leave.'

To my surprise she comes walking back toward me. I'm glad she's changed her mind.

'I'm just going exploring.' Her voice is calm. 'It's important to me, that's all,' she continues. 'And the possibility of finding others – that's important to me too. Not everything is about *you*, you know. I'm not doing any of it "*at*" you. I'm just doing it.'

CHAPTER 1

Blood seeps slowly from the skull, darkening hair and pooling on stone. The black, rushing river splashes the rocks; a tearing torrent dashing by deaf, dead ears. Night shadows wash the blue dress grey.

The body sprawls in its resting place, limbs limp, deformed by boulder-snapped bones. Icy fingers trail in the tugging water, yet unpierced by the bite of perch.

A break in the clouds reveals a pattern of printed white daisies. The blossoms crystallise like stars pricking a pitch sky.

The eyes are open, shining with moonlight, bright against the muddied, bloodied face.

AUGUST

CHAPTER 2

Zoya is watching the window. On the other side of the glass, the sparrow seems to hover, an impossible suspension, before its wings flutter and it swoops dramatically out of sight.

'So,' continues the interviewer.

Zoya's attention snaps back to the thin, grey woman and the frowning man sitting across the table, their notes neatly positioned before them in two parallel piles.

'... aside from your administrative experience,' the woman continues, 'what makes you a good fit for Charlotte Carre?'

'Well...'

Zoya's eyes flit from one serious face to the other.

'I love dance. I mean, I love to dance myself – as an amateur. I've taken a lot of dance classes, particularly over the last year, and been to see a lot of shows – er, performances.'

She looks up to the vacant patch of sky.

'I love it. It's like... the world just melts away and time itself stops... just hangs there floating...'

Zoya realises that this isn't much of a job interview answer and brings her focus back to the room – the neat furniture, pale walls and neutral expressions of the man and woman waiting for her to say something that will score some points.

'So, I just really feel that… I just think that by contributing to a – *this* – dance company, by bringing my administrative skills to the company… it would help me to feel' – she searches for the word – 'fulfilled.'

Zoya clasps her hands together neatly on her lap, straightens her spine slightly and smiles a close-lipped smile.

***

Reed's mouth hangs open, a spot of saliva pooling at the corner. As he wakes, he instinctively wipes it away with the back of his hand and then wriggles free of the tangled covers. Sitting up in bed, he reaches for the retro patterned curtain and pulls it aside to check out the morning. Sycamore trees fill the camper van window with green shadow, the leaves hanging still as a photograph. He runs his fingers through his hair. It slowly flops back into place.

Beyond the leaves lies the wide, grey suburban street and another flat August day. Nobody seems to be about. Eventually, he spies a faraway walker, circled by the curious snuffling of his dog.

Once dressed, Reed opens the cabin door, the sound soon dissipating in the quiet street. He hops onto the pavement and pulls the door shut. A car drives past the distant junction and a blackbird begins to sing somewhere, out of sight.

Reed stretches his spine, his long arms reaching toward the treetops in a wide span. He sets off on the short walk toward Dan's house, thinking about breakfast.

***

'Thank you, Miss Carmichael. That concludes the interview.'

The thin, grey woman, whose name Zoya can't remember, replaces the cap on her pen with a click.

'As mentioned,' the grumpy man adds, 'we expect to make our decision by the end of the day. Thanks for coming in.'

Zoya follows their lead in standing up, extending her arm for handshakes and exchanging polite thanks.

A loud bang at the windowpane startles her. She sees the stunned sparrow plummet to the ground, like a stone.

***

The thud of the car door sounds too loud in the quiet, still street. Dan stands on his doorstep watching Robin drive away. In the open doorway, Dan's skin prickles as cool morning air seeps into the house.

He watches as the blue Ford Fiesta quietly trundles down the street and rounds the usual corner – and he watches long after it has gone. Dan's thick, dark brows sink slowly over his stare and his pursed mouth settles in a small, pained frown.

***

In the corridor, Zoya manoeuvres herself out of the way. The thin, grey woman is calling for the next interviewee. A thin, blond woman – almost a mirror image – rises from the waiting area. Zoya notices that they embrace.

'Hi, darling – we said you'd be back!'

Zoya struggles to stash her resume in her bag and her cheeks feel hot. She stuffs the papers in and hurries down the stairs.

Hitting the open air, she turns a corner to find the back of the building and leans against the wall. She looks up through the muggy, greying skies to the windows rising above her, imagining the affectionate greetings continuing in the interview room above. She already knows that she won't be getting this job. She steps out of her uncomfortable interview shoes and flexes her feet on the grass.

***

Reed's Converse make a slight slapping sound on the drive as he ambles up to Dan's front door. The familiar suburban semi seems quiet today, no signs of life or Dan. He remembers that Sarah and Matty don't live there anymore, Dan's sister and nephew having moved in with her new boyfriend, Nathan.

He reaches for the doorbell and presses. As he waits, not hearing anything, he glances up and down the road. Someone along the street is hanging washing out to dry.

He hears faint footsteps inside the hall. Dan opens the door. He has a preoccupied look on his face.

'Reed!' Dan says, mustering an enthusiastic greeting that doesn't land quite right.

'Had you forgotten?' Reed answers, following him inside. 'We were going to go through the vanishing necklace case today…'

'No, no,' Dan says. 'You're just a bit earlier than… I suppose I lost track of time.'

They head down the hallway and into the kitchen.

'Oh, have you got company?' Reed asks. 'Is Robin still here?'

'No.'

Reed waits for the explanation, wondering what caused Dan to lose track of time. Dan intuits the unspoken question.

'I was just… thinking,' he answers.

They sit at the table.

'Right,' Dan says, planting his hands on the tabletop, 'here's what we know.'

***

Zoya leans against the wall, feeling directionless in life. As her pulse slumps back to normal, she becomes irritated by the stifling stillness of the London morning and the stiff, heavy cling of her stupid interview suit.

Not far from her feet, she sees the body of the fallen sparrow, motionless on the grass. She looks at it glumly for a few minutes, wondering what to do with the rest of her day.

Then there is a flutter. The stunned bird rights itself, takes a few faltering hops and then flies away.

*****

Sharon perches at the edge of the storeroom above the nightclub, tolerating the smell of tobacco, beer and disinfectant that has sunk deep into the walls. The room is crammed with shadowy, decrepit equipment, thick with dust and sweated grime. The music rises in muffled beats and the wasp-swarm hum echoes in the biting buzz of loose screws. One foot rests on a heavy wheel of cable, the other on the grubby floor.

The door to the office is speckled with peeling varnish and stays shut. She can't hear the men talking inside.

She peers at the paper form she is working through, resting it on the edge of an old mixing desk. She fills in the boxes of the application form in chunky capitals, glancing furtively to the corridor and the door. All she can hear is the thud of the music being played downstairs.

She works her biro carefully, filling in the bursary section, just finishing before a sixth sense tells her to check back with the office door. Her fingers scrabble to fold away the application and hurriedly stuff it out of sight in her bag. She sees the handle turn and the latch release before he emerges slowly, shoulder and hip first, still talking to the men inside.

She adjusts her position, zipping up her bag and smoothing her hair. Alex is half out of the room, still wrapping up his conversation. She sees that he is holding a bag now, one that falls with weight toward the floor. His arm looks muscular holding it. She always liked the way he stands like that; slim hips, poised for action, carrying his weight on one leg.

She tries not to wonder about the bag too much, but the thought keeps pricking her: *maybe he is finally going to pay her back.* All that money, all those years: it wasn't his, it was *hers.*

The music comes to a stop.

Alex steps fully into the corridor and looks around. Sharon stands up, making herself available.

'Sorry, babe,' he says. 'Bit of business. We're leaving now.'

Alex scoops an arm around her and nudges her forward with a hand at the small of her back. She walks ahead of him down the dark, sticky stairs.

As they move through the club below, Alex nods to all the staff. John is darting around collecting plastic glasses from the floor and Garry pauses with his broom to let them pass. They walk through the cavernous, sweat-sheened room and say goodnight to the bouncers who are crowd-managing clubbers away from the cloakroom and into the nipping, northern night. Alex and Sharon exit through the fire door.

Soon they are outside by his car, a 1977 orange Ford Capri. She watches as Alex puts the bag on the back seat.

'Babe. Hurry the fuck up,' he barks.

She opens the passenger door and glances back to the club. 'I thought we were giving Darren a lift home?'

Alex shrugs. 'Fuck him,' he says nonchalantly.

Then he leans toward her with a stern look on his face. She becomes aware that his lips are moving, that he is muttering something at her through gritted teeth. The words become clearer as his voice grows in volume and anger.

'… five, six, seven, eight…'

She cuts off his counting by quickly getting into the car.

***

My feet shuffle to the edge of the concrete. I can see the River Thames carving its wide passage through the city. I see Somerset House all lit up on the far bank and all the low, wide bridges crouching above the chill water. You cannot imagine how eerie London feels when you're the only person here.

I look at the illuminated towers in the distance and wonder what it would be like to take off from there. But this is enough.

I look to the toes of my trainers touching the void beyond the theatre roof. It's enough to get my heart pumping, faster and harder, but I'm not doing it for the adrenaline rush.

I look around at the gust-riven, empty city. I have seen it all before.

There's still a sick, cloying feeling collecting in the pit of my stomach, the sediment of a day that didn't go exactly as I'd hoped.

I think of the interview. I was clearly not their cup of tea.

I ready myself to step off now. Nothing fancy, just a step. It still shocks me; that first instant when there's no ground beneath me – just me and the fall.

I step, leaning my weight forward and soon I'm drifting head-first into the night. The air cools my face and I feel the churn of time slow around me as I fall and fall and fall…

CHAPTER 3

'Come in, Reed, come in. Good to see you! Come in,' Richard says, holding the thick, wooden door of Whale House open for him.

'Thanks,' Reed says, walking into the broad hall. 'London?' he queries, watching Richard expertly turn his wheelchair around.

They move up the shallow slope and into the body of the house.

'Yes, for a job interview with Charlotte Carre Ballet Company,' Richard explains.

'A car company?'

'Charlotte Carre – some fancy ballet school. In the office. I'm expecting her back sometime today. Come in though. It's good to see you, Reed.'

Reed walks along, onto the step-muffling carpet, following Richard through to the living room at the back. The house feels quiet. Perhaps some music is playing way up there, above them, in the parlour where Richard keeps his records, but Reed can't hear it. For a time, he felt at home here, but it's been a while. There's a different painting on the wall: an almost-finished portrait of Zoya, gifted by the artist's widow. It is absolutely her. Reed stops himself from being transfixed by it – before Richard catches him looking.

'Are you stopping for a cuppa? How have you been?'

Reed eyes the cosy plumpness of the plush sofa and chairs. The light reflecting from the flourishing garden bathes the room with shades of jade, emerald and lime.

'I, er, I can't stay long,' Reed answers, noticing something. 'Is that your book?'

A proof copy of Richard's soon-to-be-published memoir is lying on the coffee table. Richard holds it up proudly.

'*Molly and Me: Memoirs of a Zoologist*,' he quotes and immediately erupts in a scratchy chuckle. 'The publishers foisted that title on me.'

He points a finger at the old family photograph on the cover and Reed makes out a young Richard and Calliope with Molly and a tiny daughter – a child with lively hair and a happy smile. Richard chuckles again.

'Abigail's annoyed that she didn't make it onto the cover. Has insisted on "helping me" with the book tour as compensation. Somehow managed to squeeze in a small cruise for R&R in among it all... purely thinking of *me*, you understand.'

Richard finishes his book chat with a flash of his eyes and a grin.

Reed settles into an armchair by the window, looking to the greenery outside. In the garden, verdant foliage waves its branches silently at them beyond the reinforced plate glass.

'So... is Zoya coming back soon? Do you know what time? Listen, I can come back later, when she's home.'

He notices that they have planted up the outside space more like an actual garden now – now that Molly the rhino has gone. Despite the fluttering leaves, it seems empty and still out there now; nobody to munch at the bushes. He considers the scentless, silent garden beyond the glass.

'I'm a gardener now,' Richard says, noticing Reed's gaze. 'Had to do something with all that space.'

Reed finds himself looking up to the high walkway that rings the plot. He has some very pleasant memories of nights spent with Zoya up there on the veranda. It all looks so different from down here.

He can hear the swish of his fingers stroking the velvet cushion.

'You must miss her – Molly,' Reed says, but Richard doesn't answer.

Instead, he is regarding him, a knowing look to his twinkling eyes.

'I know who you mean.'

Reed suddenly feels annoyed by Richard's all-knowing scrutiny and can't help the sullen expression creeping across his own face.

'Richard,' he says, seriously, 'we're friends, okay? Me and Zoya. Friends.'

Richard nods gently and sagely. Reed's eyes flash wide.

'Friends?' Richard asks.

'Yes,' Reed replies, drawing the word out in annoyed exasperation, 'friends.'

He shifts position in the chair and fishes for his notebook, which has slipped into the crack between cushion and arm.

Richard is fun and kind and brave, but he can be really annoying sometimes, Reed thinks, stuffing the precious notebook back into his jacket.

'*Real* friends?' Richard says, pursuing his enquiry with a subtly raised brow.

Reed looks at him coolly.

'Not the type of friend just waiting around to catch her when she falls back into your arms?'

'*Yes*, Richard,' Reed insists, annoyed. 'I'm not a child. I know what friendship means.'

'Sure. It means you're there for someone even when there's nothing in it for *you*.'

'Look,' Reed says, getting to his feet, 'I just dropped by to tell her that we're going away on a job for a little while – me and Dan – so can you just tell her that for me, please? I'd do anything for her, you know that. So, can you just pass on that message, please? About me and Dan?'

Reed has stomped a couple of paces toward the door. Richard smiles, waiting for Reed to finish his rambling.

'Of course.'

Reed is standing with his hands on his hips now, his lanky frame looming over Richard's chair. He calms himself down but still feels annoyed.

'Look, I'd better go. I'm meant to be meeting him now.'

He pauses for a moment, looking again at the empty garden, then makes for the hall.

'Paranormal investigations, is it?' Richard asks, wheeling himself along behind.

Reed nods hurriedly.

'Yep. So, you'll pass on the message? I'll see myself out.'

Reed ambles down the incline and, as he opens the front door, hears Richard calling his name.

'Hey, Reed.'

Reed pauses and stops himself from rolling his eyes. He knows that Richard's heart is in the right place.

'Just make sure all this "anything" you'll be doing for her, *is* for her, and not really for *you*.'

Reed walks outside, shaking his head slightly as he goes.

'Bye, Richard,' he mutters, resigned; not looking back.

At the end of the path through the rose garden, Reed pauses to adjust the notebook he had hurriedly tucked away and discovers something unexpected. He seems to have accidentally picked up something else: the cover of *this* small notebook is plastered in a photograph of Zoya, Richard and Aunt Abigail. He stows it away again quickly, too embarrassed by the stropping off to return it right now.

Back in the safety of the Volkswagen van, buckled in and ready to go, he pulls the notebook out for another look. It's a really nice photograph. He will always be stopped in his tracks by Zoya's smile.

***

Zoya stands on the pavement, her smile spreading from ear to ear. On her way back from London, she had stopped off for a rest at Bramchester, and is mesmerised by a poster, brass-edged and important, outside the small theatre there.

She stands grinning at the discovery, but nobody else seems to care.

She doesn't notice the shuffling shoppers passing behind her, the gentle thrum of light traffic driving by, or the small dog snuffling at her feet. It sneezes as the owner drags it away.

The poster is for a dance show and the figure adorning it, photographed in a mid-air pose, is none other than Leon Foster, her favourite dancer in the whole world. The fact that his isn't exactly a household name makes this seem an even luckier find.

She checks the details at the bottom of the poster again. Yes, that's definitely today. She looks again at the blond dancer, his lean, muscular torso twisting in the leap. Then she bustles inside the theatre to find the box office, practically crossing her fingers as she goes.

***

Reed is sitting in the booth at the Little Beach Café, picking at a knot in the wooden window frame. It's too early for streetlamps in summer, but a muggy gloom seems to be descending over the town. The sky is melodramatically dark, long before sunset; stormless and strange. He watches the shadows creeping over the beach and out to sea.

Inside, the orange lights of the café reflect in shiny teapots and in sugary drops of condensation at the corners of windowpanes. There is a lull; the soporific slap of light mopping from the kitchen, tinkling cutlery at the counter and conversations easing down a gear. The softest of shadows bleeds from beneath the saucer of his cup.

The door rattles in the corner. He looks up to see Dan approaching, a funny expression on his face.

'What?' Reed says. 'You seem surprised to see me. You can't have forgotten, or you wouldn't be here.'

'No, no, I just didn't expect you to be here *yet*,' Dan says, sitting heavily on the seat opposite and slinging his jacket over the back.

'Oh… Zoya wasn't there,' Reed explains, picking off a splinter of wood. 'She's been up in London, Richard says, for a job interview.'

'So, she wants to move away?' Dan says, resuming his look of surprise. He pulls a pensive expression. 'Travelling around, wind in her hair, I can see her doing that. Living in Shilly, sand beneath her toes, I can see her doing that too – but moving to London for a job? Doesn't really seem like Zoya…'

Reed shrugs again. He notices the grain of the windowsill: twisting paths that run alongside each other, together and apart.

'She must have her reasons,' he says, though it seems like just as much of a mystery to him.

Reed stops picking at the wood and curls his hand into a ball. He forces his expression to brighten before changing the subject to the matter in hand.

'So, how are we going about this investigation?'

'Are you seeing her later?' Dan asks.

'No, I've got... plans, though.'

Reed looks at his watch.

'Actually, there's stuff I need to do.'

Dan adopts a curious expression, mouthing a silent *oh?*

This time, he sees Reed's face brighten naturally, an excited little grin appearing and disappearing, something lighting up his eyes. Reed leans forward over the table, tracing a pattern on the Formica with dancing fingers.

'I'm seeing someone.'

'You've got a date?'

'*Date*? We're not Americans, Dan. There's just... someone I've arranged to meet.' Reed watches his ice-skating fingers. 'You know Attic Books in Kembleton... on Bridge Street? Well, anyway, she works there. Lucy, she's called. You'd know her – she's always wearing colourful tights.'

He darts a small, bright, glance at Dan, unable to keep his hopes to himself.

'You sly dog,' Dan responds playfully. 'Hang on, what preparations do you need to make? I mean – no offence – but you always *look* exactly the same...'

'Effortlessly handsome, you mean?'

Dan rolls his eyes, playing along, knowing that only someone who has never considered himself a looker would make this kind of joke. He finds himself looking at his friend more observantly, though. Reed might not be what people would call handsome exactly, but when you get to know him, he has a certain, unique charm.

Dan watches Reed trying to manage his boyish excitement: changing position in his chair – the floppy hair, the glinting green eyes, the charismatic micro-expressions that flicker across his face hinting at the whirlpool of thoughts and feelings bubbling within. It's a quality that reminds him of Marcus, whose face Dan can never lay eyes on again.

'Actually,' Reed begins, apparently eager to spill the beans, 'I've got a plan. I think she might like it… I'm making her a treasure trail…'

'Like *The Goonies*?' Dan interjects.

'No, not like *The Goonies*. A treasure *trail* – not a treasure map.'

Dan is shaking his head and screwing up his face and shoulders as if to say *No, I'm not following at all.*

'So, I'm chalking out messages that will take her from the meeting place to somewhere nearby – where I'll be waiting.'

'Lying in wait?'

Dan arches a thick eyebrow.

'No. It's not *sinister*… It will be… cute. I've got these little presents for her along the way. And anyway, I think she'll like it.'

Reed nestles back into his seat. There's a low-level clinking of cutlery emanating from the other diners eating their meals.

'So, you're really moving on?' Dan asks after a moment.

'No, I've *moved* on,' Reed answers, stressing the past tense. 'Me and Zoya are just friends now. It's fine.'

'I see. Well, good. Good plan.'

'What about you? Are you seeing Robin tonight?'

Dan sighs. He looks out of the window at the darkening water.

'Yeah.'

Reed stops fidgeting.

'What?'

Dan screws up his face again. He takes a breath but the words that follow tumble slowly from his lips.

'I think I'm breaking up with him.'

He opens his eyes to check Reed's response.

'I thought it was going well?'

'I'm not sure we're in it for the right reasons.'

Reed waits for Dan to say more.

'*I'd* lost someone... *He'd* lost someone... Look, the only reason we know him in the first place is because he wanted to meet the people who discovered Donna's body... And it's probably too soon after...'

He doesn't say the name.

Reed can see his point but doesn't comment – only Dan and Robin can know. Dan doesn't seem to want to talk about it anymore.

'So,' Reed says, getting back to business, 'it's a rare bookshop, up in Bramchester...'

Dan accepts the prompt.

'Right. Run by two sisters who live above the shop. Can't see they've anything to gain from the story of a vanishing necklace but, we'll see, won't we?'

'Are we taking the usual kit?'

'Yep, all checked – all present and correct.'

'So, if we want to be there by eleven, we should leave at…?'

'Say… nine?' Dan suggests.

'Nine's fine,' Reed says. 'You never know, I might be having a late night.'

Reed flashes his eyebrows in pantomime emphasis, meaning his date.

Dan cocks his head slightly.

'You know, most men might consider taking her for a dinner or to a show…'

***

Inside Bramchester Theatre Royal, the audience is filling up. Zoya sits between empty seats, people-watching in happy anticipation. Of the couples, companions and small groups filling up the rows, nobody seems to be quite as excited as *she* feels. She picks up the programme, taking out the insert for a closer look.

There, on a small advert the size of a bookmark, she reads about a residential project that the dance company apparently runs. Somewhere near Kedbury, near the Welsh border, she thinks. Her eyes skip to the part about open auditions and then flicker back over it again.

The orchestra finishes the warm-up and the house lights grow dim.

Zoya slips the advert into her bag and settles back in her chair. There is a gentle hush, then the curtain rises. Music starts and spotlights find a lone figure on the stage.

Unusual modernist music begins to grow; like a heartbeat that matches her own. The dancer pulses with the beat, his hair, golden in the light. And then there are shapes and balances and stretches that make him seem gravity-defying. And then there are pulses that pull him earthbound and human again; contradictory phases that she understands – but couldn't explain.

Zoya has seen him perform on stage before, but she wasn't sitting so close. She watches his face for a while, turning through beams of light, but it is the dancing that draws her in. She stops thinking and sinks into it.

Somehow, she feels great affinity for the way he moves, as if he is expressing something that she, herself, feels inside. Somehow, she knows that she would dance it that way too, *is* dancing it now.

Sitting alone in the dark, Zoya completely loses herself, falling, ever falling, into the dancer and the dance. The world melts away and she floats in the air with him.

C H A P T E R 4

'Hi, Dad, it's me.'

Zoya is leaning on the wall of the telephone recess in the bed and breakfast in Bramchester. The small alcove is fringed in painted plywood and decorated with seventies wallpaper – a green and aubergine pattern embellished with motifs like furling leaves.

'Hi, love. So, how was the show? Worth the detour?'

His voice is warm and clear through the earpiece.

'Yes, it was… I loved it.'

'Great. Are you coming home today?'

Zoya turns and raises the audition flyer that she is clutching in her hand.

'Actually…'

There is a creak as she leans her knee on the shiny, red velvet bench. She doesn't sit down.

'What is it? You got the job with Charlotte Carre?'

'Oh, no. But there's this… opportunity.' She smiles nervously. 'It's a dance project, Dad.'

'Oh?'

Her eyes flicker greedily over the description, although she has read it a thousand times.

'Open Dance Project – New Movement School. It says they are open to anyone, not looking for experienced dancers, no age limit, just people with passion and determination.'

'When are the auditions?'

'Tonight!'

'What are you going to do?'

'They don't even want you to prepare something – just take along some music you like and dance.'

'Sounds a lot more fun than keeping the books for ballet dancers, honey.'

'I know. Oh, Dad, *I'd* be dancing!'

'Go for it, love. Good luck!'

She runs her finger down the flyer.

'*Passionate and determined*,' she quotes, 'I can be that!'

***

Reed pulls the van into the small car park opposite their destination; a row of assorted buildings seamed together with shop fronts at the pavement.

'Here we are,' he says, turning off the engine and pulling the handbrake on.

They scan the row identifying it: Popplewell's Rare Books – then turn to one another.

'You sure you don't want to fortify yourself with a coffee before we go in?' Dan asks.

'No. Let's just get started. Do you think they're in?'

The rare-book shop presents large Edwardian windows, symmetrically flanking a deep-set door, but they are so crammed with shelving that the interior looks shadowy and dark. The shallow bay windows on the floor above are shrouded in smoggy lace curtains and it is impossible to see any signs of life inside.

They sit in the van, looking, not moving from their seats.

'We *are* expected,' Dan confirms, checking his watch for time. 'So, *did* you have a late night last night?'

Reed leans back on the headrest.

'No, it was disappointingly early.'

'*How* early?' asks Dan, though that's not really what he means.

'*Very* early,' Reed answers, rolling his eyes to cast a dark look at Dan.

Dan picks up on his meaning: very early, and not in a good way.

'Lucy-with-the-tights wasn't impressed by your trail of whimsy, then? What happened?'

'She just' – Reed cringes at the memory – 'had this *look* on her face, you know?'

'Terrified, you mean?' Dan asks, only half-joking.

'No, not *terrified*, just...' Reed thinks for a minute. 'She politely told me she thinks I might be a bit too weird for her...'

'You *are* weird.'

'So, what about you? We've been driving for two hours and you haven't said anything about Robin yet. Was he upset?'

'No, he was... understanding. It was horrible.'

Reed rolls his head on the headrest to face Dan.

'Said he'd give me some space to figure things out,' Dan continues. 'Said it was probably a good thing I was going away for a bit…'

Reed looks up and down the street ahead of them, blowing a small breath between his lips.

'Fucking understanding, perfect-for-you little shit,' he jokes. Then he looks at Dan more seriously. 'He's right though, isn't he?'

'No, there's nothing to figure out.'

The two men sit there for a few moments longer. There are still no signs of life in the shop or the flat above.

'So, if this is anything like the Bradbury case, there'll be some kind of safe or storeroom, that isn't what – or is *more* than – it seems. But, as always…'

Dan pauses and Reed picks up on his prompt.

'… we'll be keeping open minds.'

'Right.' Dan claps his palms to his thighs. '*I'll* do the talking; let's go in.'

CHAPTER 5

In the parlour above the shop, Minnie Popplewell is pointing a finger at Dan.

'Tea?' she asks, checking his order.

Dan nods.

'Coffee?'

She points her finger at Reed.

'Black, please.'

Minnie bustles briskly out of the living room and into the adjoining kitchen, her thick cords rasping as she walks.

They are in an old-fashioned sitting room, both fussy and functional, featuring a finely patterned chintz settee stitched solidly into a carved, wooden frame. A heavy urn containing peacock feathers stands by the dark fireplace, a vase of dried flowers on the sideboard behind the settee.

Dan settles back into the armchair, exchanging a polite smile with the other sister, Laverne. Reed looks around.

The ornaments decorating the room demand closer inspection; they're both inviting and foreboding at the same time. Reed is drawn to a model ship, sailing to nowhere in a rectangular glass case, but doesn't dare touch it. Instead, he turns his attention to the miniature globe beside it, spinning it slowly with his finger and peering at the old country boundaries and names.

He goes to stand by the fireplace, the tasselled rug tangling under his feet. The clock on the mantelpiece ticks so quietly that Reed can only hear it when he leans in. He picks up a small hunting dog ornament, the wood tooled to form a keenly observed coat.

Laverne Popplewell looks nervously from one visitor to the other, throwing furtive glances to the doorway through which her sister disappeared. She smooths her long skirt over her knees and leans forward in her seat. It looks like she is about to say something, so Dan instinctively leans toward her to listen, causing the leather chair to creak.

Reed sets down the wooden dog, straightens his pose and listens.

Laverne opens her mouth to talk.

'Right!' Minnie announces, striding back into the room. 'Kettle's on.'

Laverne sits back in her seat.

'Thanks for coming, Mr Mather and er…' Her wavering gesture in Reed's direction is so fleeting that he doesn't have time to supply his name again. 'Right. So, this damned necklace of ours.'

She tugs on her trousers at the thigh before sitting at the other end of the sofa from her sister. Laverne is now looking down at her hands, fiddling with some of her rings.

'I'm afraid you've arrived at a time when it isn't here. Or perhaps that's good for your investigation?' She flexes an eyebrow angularly. 'Up to you. Up to you. In any case, I'll give you the rundown about the thing.'

'And it's not here because it…' Dan asks, trailing off in a leading way.

Minnie levels a plain look at him.

'… has vanished?' Reed suggests, trying to sound more credulous than he can yet muster, ambitions to keep an open mind or not.

'Well, exactly,' Minnie says. 'Ah!'

Having heard the kettle boiling, she rises again and leaves the room.

Dan and Reed slowly pivot expectant faces from the doorway toward Laverne. She smiles bashfully then leans toward them again.

'She thinks it's me,' Laverne whispers.

Dan's eyes widen.

'Right. Tea's just steeping. Now, where were we?' Minnie says, interrupting the whispers. Minnie sits again, resting her forearms on her knees and clapping her hands together in a sturdy grip. 'Oh now. Did you want biscuits? Up to you. Laverne would you…?'

After a brief pause, Laverne begins to move.

'Of course.'

Laverne springs from the sofa, smooths her skirt, and glides out of the room.

Minnie sits motionless, watching her sister as she vacates the room with a measured, tracking swivel of her eyes.

When Laverne is out of earshot, Minnie proceeds in a controlled voice, quietened for the purpose of discretion but without a hint of Laverne's breathy whisper.

Reed wants to exchange a glance with Dan but controls the instinct. He leans against the wall.

'Now. Just a word of warning. My sister is quite sensitive about that necklace. Might affect how you handle this. Up to you. Up to you. Anyway, it might surprise people to know, but it was I who commissioned you. Not my sister. Even though she's much more…' She lets the sentence hang for a second. 'But you're scientists, aren't you? That's why I called.'

She sits back and rests her palms on her thighs.

Reed really wonders what Dan is making of this but can't see his expression from where he stands.

Laverne enters with a tray of drinks and biscuits accompanied by a gentle smile. Once the tray has been set down on the coffee table, milk poured, sugar stirred and thanks uttered, Dan begins his questions.

'Okay, so if you could describe what has been going on…'

He makes sure he looks at each sister equally, but it is, of course, Minnie who takes the floor.

'This necklace is something we keep for sentimental reasons, you understand, of no great value. Sometimes it is in the safe where we left it and sometimes it isn't. It comes and goes. Now. I know what you're thinking – we are just misplacing the damned thing, getting confused, something like that – but I can assure you, we are *not*.' She takes a swift drink from her teacup. '*I* am the only person with the combination to that safe – and I change it regularly – and I can assure you that *I* don't remove the necklace and I *don't* put it back.'

Dan flips open his notebook.

'You are the only person who knows the combination to the safe?' he repeats, scribbling.

The sound of his pencil scrawling across the paper is audible in the quiet room. Laverne makes a staring expression at this, silently sending the investigators a message with her eyes: *I told you so.*

Dan sees her in his peripheral vision but doesn't let on. Laverne fingers the silk scarf that is luxuriously draped around her neck, with small, fidgety strokes.

'But it's not there at the moment?'

'No.'

'And could you perhaps describe the necklace?'

'Better than that. We've a photograph.' She turns to Laverne. 'Didn't you bring it through? Never mind. I'll fetch it.'

Minnie dashes away to do just that.

'I told you.'

Their attention snaps to Laverne.

'Why?' Dan asks.

'Well, there was this one time she caught me with it, trying to contact the spirit world…'

Dan and Reed give her different versions of the same encouraging yet unconvinced smile.

'A sort of séance, you know.'

'And who were you trying to contact?' Dan asks, his voice even more of a whisper.

'There!' Minnie's voice booms from the doorway. She strides around the coffee table to thrust a pewter-framed photograph in front of Dan. 'That's Phoebe. She's wearing it in this photograph. You can get quite a good look at it. Up to you.'

Dan takes the frame from her outstretched grip and looks at the picture.

There are three women arranged in a composition by the studio photographer – maybe ten years ago. The woman in the middle is wearing a necklace decorated with a bird and some other shapes.

'That's a hummingbird. Various flora. Steel. Enamel. Silver plate.'

'And Phoebe is…?'

'Phoebe was our sister,' Laverne explains softly. 'We were originally three.'

'I see.'

Dan recognises the family resemblance in the photograph now, although the sisters look quite different: Laverne draped in one of her scarves; Minnie sporting her bob; Phoebe with her rounder face and chunky necklace and barely contained laugh.

'That's why we keep the damned thing, you know,' Minnie adds, appearing for the first time more flapped than unflappable.

Laverne reaches out a thin arm to touch Minnie comfortingly on the shoulder. Minnie looks at her, blinking. It is the first time that Reed has seen them make eye contact since they arrived.

'Minnie doesn't really like to see the necklace,' Laverne softly explains.

'But I don't want it to go astray,' Minnie adds in a forceful tone of voice.

'I see,' Dan says, gently. 'Can I ask why you are the only one with the combination to the safe?'

He gestures with his stubby pencil, implying that he is only asking for the record.

'It's just business. I run the books and keep the paperwork in order. Laverne is really our buyer – she goes out and finds treasures to stock the shop. Couldn't do it without her. But the office is my domain really. I keep things in order.'

'I see.'

Dan closes his notebook.

'So – if it's okay with you – I'm going to start with a search of the shop.' He holds up his hand in a placatory gesture. 'That's not to say we don't believe you, or we're closed to the possibility that Phoebe's necklace is actually dematerialising. It's just… the process…'

'Up to you. Up to you.'

Reed unfolds his arms and moves away from the wall.

'I'll get the metal detector from the…'

Reed's sentence trails off as he notices Laverne staring at him. She rises from her seat and moves across the room toward him.

'You…' she says.

She keeps advancing. Reed finds his back against the wall.

'You have such an… *aura* around you. You must let me…'

She lifts her face toward his, looking deeply into his eyes. Reed swallows.

'What?'

'… read your cards.'

'Okay,' Dan says, quickly slipping from the armchair and making for the door, 'I'll go get the detector. Reed, you stay here and… discover your destiny.'

***

Downstairs in the office at the back of the shop, Dan and Minnie are standing in front of an old gunmetal-grey safe. The door has been opened and Dan is cramming as much of his head and shoulders into the space as will fit. He is tapping his way across the interior surfaces while Minnie talks.

'She had it with her in the middle of a Ouija board or something like that. Had all the candles and crystals and so on. I don't know what she was expecting to happen but, well… we had quite an argument about that.'

'Right. And does Laverne engage in that sort of thing often? Would you mind passing me my torch?'

'Up to you,' Minnie says, handing it to him. 'No, nothing like that. The odd bit of tarot reading. Mild spiritual stuff. Nothing like trying to summon *ghosts*.'

Dan clicks off the torch, having found nothing unusual about the construction of the safe, and emerges, accidentally knocking his head.

'Ow. Right. So. Here's the plan for our investigation. I'll conduct a search of the premises – with your permission – to eliminate the possibility of the item simply having been misplaced.' He looks at her. 'Elimination. You understand...'

'Permission granted.'

'And then we'll set up our kit around the safe, get some readings and take it from there.'

'Up to you,' Minnie says, by way of assent.

'And, if you don't mind – for the purposes of elimination – I'd like to reset the combination – temporarily – so that I am the only one who knows... Is that alright? You might want to remove any items from the safe beforehand – that you need or...'

'I see. For the purposes of elimination. Yes, I quite understand. Up to you.'

***

A short while later, Dan is ready to explore the cramped aisles of the bookshop with his metal detector. The place is like a maze. He sets to work, venturing into the claustrophobic warren of bookshelves that fill the shop floor. It could be some time before he can move his exploration to the living quarters upstairs.

He works methodically, sweeping the detector over every mountainous facade of books, easing his bulk around tight corners and into the narrow spaces and confusing side rooms, learning to look for small, unexpected, trip-causing steps.

At least the ceiling is quite high, or the musk of old paperbacks and destabilising ink might be overwhelming. And at least everything is shelved neatly in this shop – Minnie, he suspects, keeping everything shipshape.

Dan stops to flex his tiring arm a moment, clenching and un-clenching his fist to keep the blood flowing and to counteract the prick of pins and needles in his hand. Still, he's glad he left Reed upstairs as he would only have got under his feet here; getting distracted by mysterious volumes, reading the spines, thumbing through countless yellowed paperbacks. Maybe he will learn something upstairs.

Carefully, he lifts the detector head to sweep the next shelf, and hears the ticking, creaking cackle in his headphones surge to a shrill, chirping squawk. He fingers through the contents of the shelf, plucking an old-style five pence piece from between the books and slipping it into his pocket, where it jangles with the other coins, paperclips and screws.

***

'Ah. The Wanderer,' Laverne says, laying out another card.

Reed looks at her, wondering if she picked it because she has seen his camper van parked outside.

'I'll be embarking on a journey, do you predict?'

'Not literally. The Wanderer is about open hearts and trust. See the cliff edge and the rainbow path?'

She looks him in the eye.

'For *you,* this is about stepping out and taking a risk.'

'Right.'

'You don't believe in any of this, do you?' she asks, sinking in her posture, though her voice remains happy enough.

'Well, one thing I'm learning... is to keep an open mind.'

Reed takes another sip of his cooling coffee, pleased to have discovered this all-purpose phrase.

'You know that I don't believe in ghosts or anything?' Laverne says. 'Tarot is different. That one time – that Minnie found me with Phoebe's necklace – that was just a one-off. I was in the full flow of grief and... quite desperate, I suppose.'

Reed can't help but believe her.

'And when did she...?'

'Nearly three years ago now. A car crash – not her fault. It was a selfish... stupid... selfish young man who...' Her emotion quells. 'And I miss her every day. Always laughing, she was. We don't laugh so much now.'

'I'm sorry.'

Laverne smiles at him and her gaze wanders to the photograph of the three sisters which has now been placed on the side table.

'I don't have any family,' Reed finds himself saying.

'Then I'm sorry too. Friends though,' she says, tapping on the Three of Cups card already laid on the table between them.

And not many of those, he thinks, but remains silent, a slight wrinkle forming on his brow.

Laverne turns over another card and places it in the final space.

'The Empress,' she says. She looks over the array of tarot cards and adopts the broadest of smiles. 'Unconditional love.'

'*For* me… or *from* me?'

Laverne's smile breaks into a small, tinkling laugh.

'Only time will tell.'

Just then, Dan appears in the doorway clutching the metal detector, the headphones encircling his neck.

He smiles at Laverne politely, then adopts a grumpier expression specifically for Reed.

'Thanks for your help, Reed…' he says dryly.

Reed gestures to the coffee table and the tarot cards.

'But you said…'

'Anyway, I've done with the shop downstairs – it isn't there. Time to check over the flat.' He looks at Laverne. 'Oh, Minnie said that this would be alright…? She's going to supervise…'

'Yes, yes, of course. It's time for my constitutional. I like to take a turn around the park.'

She gathers the tarot deck and stands, smoothing her skirt.

'If you'll excuse me.'

After Laverne has left them alone, Dan fixes Reed with a wry, lopsided grin.

'So, what does your future hold?'

'I'm going to meet a tall, dark stranger…' Reed jokes.

Dan opens his arms in a theatrical gesture.

'Ta da! Here I am! Right, let's get to work.'

That evening Zoya is sitting on a wooden chair, turning a cassette tape over and over in her hands.

Sitting in the corridor makes her feel like she is back at school. The halls are longer here but it's the same vibe: vinyl flooring, noticeboards, chunky radiators, breeze-block walls.

The door into the hall where the auditions are taking place features a small window but it's too high for Zoya to see much from her seat. She can only hear the loud classical music blasting from some stereo, and no voices or other clues. The wooden seat next to hers is vibrating against the metal frame.

She seems to be the last to audition – at least, she's the only person waiting in the corridor.

She listens to the orchestral music. She looks down at her cassette – a compilation spooled to the start of a particular track on Side A. She begins tapping her fingers on the plastic casing.

The woman from the dance school looks up from her paperwork, smiles professionally and then gets back to her task.

Zoya watches her, waiting to make eye contact.

'It said to bring a piece of music we like…?'

'That's right,' the woman answers, looking up and smiling again.

'And we didn't have to prepare a routine?'

The woman sets down her pen.

'No, they're not looking for accomplished dancers – it's more about your style, energy, spirit, potential… That sort of thing.'

Zoya nods; the movement veers close to rocking in her chair.

'Have you had many people?' Zoya asks.

'A few. And we're holding open auditions in the north too.'

The classical music in the hall comes to a stop. Come to think of it, there was classical music playing in there when Zoya first arrived too. She turns the cassette tape over. She doesn't have any classical music on there, but Side B starts with a film soundtrack that's a bit more… well, a bit *less*…

Now, she hears a man's muffled voice from inside the room and wonders if it's Leon Foster. Her insides flutter. She hopes that it is him – *and* that it's not. At least, they know we're *meant* to be amateurs, she thinks.

She rummages in her bag quickly and finds a band to tie back her hair. The door to the hall opens and closes as the previous auditionee exits and escapes down the squeaking corridor.

'Can I ask you a quick question?' Zoya asks the woman.

'Yes?'

'PJ Harvey or Vangelis?'

'Is that world music?' the woman asks.

World music! Zoya thinks, annoyed at the assumption.

'Never mind,' she says, neutrally.

The woman is looking through the small window into the hall.

'They're ready for you,' she says, smiling and opening the door.

Zoya walks in, trying to convey energy rather than nerves. She sees three people sitting behind long tables and a large space cleared of chairs. None of the people seems to be Leon Foster.

A man has risen from the note-strewn table and is coming toward her. He introduces everyone but Zoya doesn't really take in who's who.

'What's your name?' asks the older woman checking the list in front of her.

'Zoya Carmichael.'

'Are you warmed up?' asks the man.

'Yes.'

'Is this your music?' he is asking, holding out a hand for Zoya's tape.

'Yes.'

He takes it over to the cassette player at the side of the room.

'Now remember – Zoya – just have fun with it. We're not interested in routines,' another woman is saying.

'Which side is it?' the man with the tape asks.

Zoya swallows and changes her mind about the PJ Harvey track. Too edgy, too... verse, chorus, verse. At least the *Blade Runner* music is more... 'expressive dance'.

Maybe she shouldn't be dancing to music from a film, though. Maybe they won't know what it is.

'Start of Side B, please.'

The man rewinds the tape as Zoya takes a spot in the middle of the cleared space, glad they haven't got her up on the small stage. She can feel three pairs of eyes on her and her heart beats faster. The music swells loudly through the hall and then she starts to move.

***

I find myself back at the school for some reason tonight.

The school gate opens with a resonant clang and I walk across the empty playground, bypassing a scatter of spilled salty crisps. One cracks under my tread.

I pass the canteen block and find the fire escape. The metal steps sing as I climb. My feet sound a percussive beat that rings out in the empty night-time like a glockenspiel scale.

At the top, I take a look around. The suburban street-lamps light a sweep of semi-detached houses that fold themselves around a street plan, their tiled roofs lining the road, two by two. Away from the sea, not even a near-by river, the empty night sounds dead. There is not even enough wind to ruffle the small trees in the gardens.

I take a look at the guttering and try to assess whether the roof will allow for a nice climb. I think I can proba-bly get up there, using the railing and the ventilation box but, actually, I don't have the energy. Physically, yes – the dreaming always makes things easy – but mentally, no.

I try not to dwell on the audition, but I can see the windows of the school hall from here.

Maybe I'm not as passionate and determined as I thought I could be. I wish I'd danced to the other side of the tape. Doesn't matter. I'm probably not the right fit anyway. Would have been good though, a year of dancing with them.

I look down to the playground, now several storeys below. This is fine. I don't need to get up on the rooftop. I can have my fall from here. I've been training myself to experience more of the fall before it makes me wake up and the thought does cross my mind that this might not be high enough – maybe I'll stay in the dreaming all the way to the bottom and experience the crunching crash when my head meets the ground.

I would still wake up fine, though, in my bed in the B&B. I don't see how I *couldn't* because I'm not really *here*. I'd rather not *feel* like I'm hitting the asphalt though. Well, I'm doing it, either way.

I climb up onto the metal railing and lift my legs over the side. And, because there's nothing to see, when I let go, I close my eyes.

CHAPTER 7

Zoya walks into a small café on the high street, as much for something to do as for a drink. She likes the name – Planet Oeuf; very clever. Maybe she could be in the mood to eat some eggs.

It looks to be a popular café, furnished with plain wooden tables and featuring an exposed brick wall. The place is brightened by yellow paint and hung with quirky pictures. As she enters, she is enveloped by the aroma of steaming coffee, sizzling bacon and the blossoming sweetness of the cakes and scones on display. The happy clatter of customers tucking in and catching up welcomes her further in.

There, toward the back of the room, she notices a couple of very familiar shapes. A big man and a wiry man are sitting at a round table, expansive and hunched respectively, but both leaning toward one another, a discussion underway.

She pauses her pace and smiles to herself. As she nears their table, she can hear what Dan is saying.

'So, last night's readings indicate that there's some electrical device in the office, but I didn't spot it…'

'A bug?' suggests Reed.

'Could be,' responds Dan, 'but, unless Minnie is saying the safe combination aloud to herself when she changes it, I don't know what use that would be…'

Zoya has stopped by their table but they haven't noticed her yet. Reed is fidgeting with the salt and pepper pots, triangulating them with the small flower vase.

'Shhh or someone might hear you…' she says, smiling when they look up.

'Zoya!' Dan says. 'What are the chances?'

He looks from her to Reed. Reed pulls a tiny expression that tells Dan he wasn't expecting to see her either, but, Dan notices, he also starts radiating that same glow he gets whenever she's around.

'Are you joining the team?' Dan asks, pulling out a wooden chair for her. 'We're professional paranormal investigators now.'

'I heard,' she says, sitting down. 'How's it going?'

Reed nods a few times.

'Good. We've got a case nearby.' He lowers his voice to a whisper. 'The case of the vanishing necklace.'

Zoya laughs a little and Reed mirrors her infectious giggle with his flickering smile.

'So, what are you doing here?' he asks, looking from eye to eye. 'Your dad said you were in London.'

'Oh, just a detour. Had to see a man about a dance project…'

'So,' Dan says, 'it's another job?'

'Hmmm, sort of. I don't want to say anymore – don't want to jinx my chances.'

She picks up a laminated menu, trying to decide if she wants something to eat.

'So, is it based here?' Reed asks.

'No, somewhere near Kedbury – Falconshire, is it?' She shrugs. 'Somewhere near Wales anyway. It would be for a year. And Dad and Abigail are going to be away, flitting back and forth on the…'

Her words trail off as she considers the menu.

'… the book tour?' Reed supplies.

Zoya nods.

'I forgot you two were telepathic,' Dan jokes, adding an expression that asks someone to explain.

'It's his memoir that's coming out. Seems to be generating some buzz!' Zoya says.

'Well… Africa, your mum, you, rhinos, Geddle Zoo, Gamstorp disease, Molly saving his life, catching a murderer… I can see why,' Reed says, secretly thinking how he hasn't achieved anything with his own life.

'Hello, what can I get you?'

The three friends look up to see a waitress, ready with her pencil and pad.

'A tea please, sweetheart,' Dan says.

'Black coffee. Please,' adds Reed.

Zoya glances up from the laminated menu.

'Could I have a cappuccino, please?' she asks. 'And a "breakfast omelette"?'

Dan and Reed look at one another, nodding slightly.

'Breakfast omelettes all round,' Dan says, making a small loop with his pointing finger.

The waitress finishes her jotting with a neat full stop, smiles and returns to the kitchen.

'So,' Zoya begins, placing her palms on the tablecloth, 'is it a poltergeist, do you think?'

Reed knows that *she* knows that *nobody* at the table believes that poltergeist are a thing – but he likes that she is taking an interest.

'So, it's like this,' Dan answers, 'either there's an actual vanishing necklace or…'

'… or some human is stealing it from the safe,' Reed says, finishing Dan's sentence.

'Hmmmm,' Zoya responds, putting an exaggerated thinking-finger to her lips as if to pretend that both options seem valid.

Reed and Zoya smile at one another with just their eyes.

'But we don't know how they're doing it…' Dan says.

'… yet,' adds Reed.

'And people pay you to poke around in their lives like this?' Zoya asks.

A quick flash of her gaze toward his tells Reed that she is thinking about him secretly poking around people's lives in the dreaming – but she wouldn't say anything about it in front of Dan.

'Are you worried about your dance thing?' Reed asks.

Zoya looks at her fingers.

'Had my audition last night. Just waiting to hear back.'

When she raises her gaze, she sees that they are still watching her.

'I just feel like it could be what I need.'

She pats a short rhythm on the table and looks out at the street.

'They must be able to see that you're better than a Zwiffle other dancers!' Reed says encouragingly.

He has seen her dance.

'A *Zwiffle*?' she queries, one brow raised.

Reed shrugs innocently.

'It's a number!' he insists, simply, even though it's blatantly not.

'And *that's* why *I* take care of all the maths in this outfit,' Dan says.

'So, what does Reed bring to the party?' she asks, not looking at the man she knows can literally go anywhere in his dreams.

'He helps out in other ways… knows his way around the kit now…'

'I stop Dan getting lonely,' Reed quips, 'like a pet.'

Zoya chuckles but understands that this isn't entirely a joke. She imagines them on the long road trip they took last year: Reed turning up the radio, his fingers tapping on the steering wheel, Dan in mourning and nursing a broken arm.

She also remembers the nights that she and Reed spent together in that van.

The waitress arrives at their table and transfers their drinks from her tray: one tea, one black coffee, one cappuccino.

They thank her and she walks away.

Zoya finds herself closest to the sugar bowl, so she picks up the spoon.

'Still one for you?' she asks Reed.

He nods and she adds the spoon of sugar to his drink.

'One for me,' she mutters, narrating her actions. 'Dan?'

'One for me, too.'

***

After a day of wasting time in and around Bramchester – looking through charity shops, a long walk by the canal – Zoya returns to her bed and breakfast.

She stops at the reception desk and rings the small bell with trepidation.

'Hi, have there been any messages for me?'

'Miss Carmichael?' the receptionist asks, reaching for something in a pigeonhole.

'Ms.'

'Pardon?'

'Doesn't matter. Thanks.'

He hands her a small envelope, like in the movies. She takes it, already feeling disappointed – she's going to have to deal with what they thought of her, now.

Turning away, she rips open the envelope and fishes out the note from inside. She reads the message and then reads it again. The worried expression doesn't ease from her brow.

She walks down the hallway to the telephone alcove and dials the phone number written on the note.

She taps the phone absent-mindedly as it rings.

'Hello? Hi, this is Zoya Carmichael. I… got your message, I…'

'Ah yes, Zoya, we'd love it if you could come back for a second audition. The same time and place – tomorrow night?'

Zoya takes a breath. Her pulse begins racing.

'I'll be there!'

***

In a graffitied telephone box – the one around the corner, out of sight – Sharon is dropping coins into the slot.

A few cars pass at the far junction between the brick terraces and the block of grimy bungalows. Some kids are booting a ball on the rubbish-scattered waste ground nearby, occasionally hitting the rusted remains of a spindly goalpost with a crash.

She drops in the final coin.

Wind shoots through the broken pane like icy breath on her neck, but the blast is welcome because otherwise, the phone box smells of marijuana and piss.

Then she carefully dials the number written on a crumpled piece of paper in her hand. She hears the ringing tone at the other end and looks around; along the street behind her and then back toward the corner that leads to the house. It is late afternoon now, but *he* is in there asleep.

'Hi, yes, this is Sharon Surtees. I'm calling about my audition for… yes… yes… yes, thank you. And the thing itself is going to be in Falconshire?'

She thinks the county is someplace down south, past Birmingham at least. *The further away, the better*, she thinks.

'And I just wanted to check – you got my bursary form? Yes. Yes – thank you,' she says hurriedly, hanging up the phone.

I'll be there, she thinks – but first she will have to figure out *how*.

***

I'm standing in the middle of the shop. The amber streetlamps render the bookshelves a strange, alien landscape. The vintage scents seem stronger by night.

I tiptoe carefully through the aisles, peering at my feet to make sure I don't knock anything flying – including myself. I reach the door to the office and listen for a long minute. A necklace thief might not be able to see *me* behind the fog of this dreaming dimension – but they would be able to see the door, first closed, then open and out of place.

I let myself in. We have set up our meters again tonight – but without holding a vigil. The culprit would definitely stay away with us two sitting right there.

I do wonder, though, if I will catch something happening: that sense of things moving just beyond my peripheral vision, of things having changed when I look again. But, for the five minutes I stand there by the safe, nothing happens, and nothing feels weird.

I turn to the passageway and the stairs that lead up to the parlour, feeling in my pocket for my torch.

I enter the quiet room – it is perfectly empty, I can just tell. I flick on the torch and allow the weak beam to cast diffused light on the objects I have already seen, and then help me to scrutinise the contents of the cupboards and drawers.

I take my methodical sweep through into the kitchen – finding no necklace – and then reacquaint myself with Phoebe's vacant bedroom. Many of her possessions are still there, although she has been dead a few years now. We looked through everything earlier and, to be honest, her room – all preserved and kept how she liked it – felt much spookier in the waking world.

I remember the room in daylight: crisp, clean, lavender bed sheets, one corner turned down ready for someone who will never come. We had been allowed to open the curtains and let the light in, and the thick, heavy swish reminded me of stage curtains opening onto a set.

I remember the vanity unit still set with a tray. I noticed a small perfume bottle, its contents long since evaporated. The heavy drawers still ran smoothly, opening to clean, pressed clothing with a sigh.

The best discovery was a small banjo but when I plucked a string, I found it was out of tune. Minnie had frowned and left the room at that point, but I meant no disrespect. The saddest thing was the paperback on the bedside table, a bookmark showing the pages which will never be read.

Tonight, the peace of her bedroom envelops me – because it's the same peace I feel in every night-place, everywhere I go.

Next comes Minnie's bedroom. I can tell by the glimpse of flat pyjama sleeve that she is sleeping right there. By now, after all these years of snooping – all those finger-rifling searches through all those homes – I can tell when a pile of clothes indicates a sleeping person and when it's just a pile of clothes.

I'm really efficient at this. And, this time, I have the baseline of a fully sanctioned, thorough daytime search to go on. I'm basically checking to see if anything is different – like an elaborate memory game – attuned to any sudden appearance of the hummingbird necklace, or anything else that seems weird.

Minnie's bedroom is just as it was in the daytime – all her neat stores of possessions very much the same.

The next room is the bathroom and there is so little to check through that it doesn't take very long at all. I unscrew the shower head, look in and behind the cistern, shake and squeeze the bottles of toiletries to feel for anything metal that might be cunningly hidden inside.

That leaves Laverne's room and I see it almost as soon as I step through the door. The slight chink of light that slips between the curtains makes it twinkle on the pillow: surely, the missing necklace. I creep closer toward her – or the place where I know she must be; another sleeping sister. I recognise the nightdress that we saw folded on top of the eiderdown earlier. I look down at the bed. It is unmistakeable. There lies Laverne – and she is wearing the hummingbird necklace as she sleeps.

CHAPTER 8

The next morning, Zoya is making another call.

'Hi, Dad, it's me.'

'Hi, love. How did it go?'

'Well... They want me to go back for a second audition... tonight.'

'That's great, love, well done.'

'Yeah...'

'What's wrong? I thought you were excited about it?'

'I... was.'

'What is it? Cold twinkletoes?'

Zoya laughs.

'I don't know. I was just thinking, I mean, I was happy staying in Shilly, living at home... before. This would be living somewhere near... Kedbury? And... maybe this isn't for me... or I'm not for them. They probably won't even offer me a place so...'

'Well, love, there's no right or wrong choice about this. Doesn't matter what other people say – only you can decide what's right for you. But maybe...'

'Maybe what?'

'Maybe you can do the deciding *after* they offer you a place?'

Zoya nods and laughs.

'You're right. I should go and audition first.'

'Dancing tonight, thinking tomorrow,' Richard says, summarising.

'I *will* go.'

***

In the old part of town, above the bookshop, two sisters and two paranormal investigators are gathered around the coffee table.

Reed notices that Laverne is wearing a different silk scarf today: cream with tumbling feathers.

'So, there it is,' Dan says, nudging a thin paper report across the table. 'It's basically just as I've explained in the rundown, but with a summary of the data we collected should you be interested in seeing the details…'

'Ah. Data,' Minnie says. 'Just the thing.'

It doesn't sound like she's joking.

Dan sits back in the leather armchair and raises his hands in a gesture of splay-fingered honesty.

'We didn't find your lost necklace and there's nothing unusual about the safe.'

Although they'd picked up a slight electrical reading, it didn't lead anywhere, so there was no need to overplay it. He just put it down to old wiring in the house. The tribo-scope had taken a wobbly at one point, during that second night, but that couldn't be linked to anything either, so Dan didn't point it out. They hadn't found anything that helped to solve the case.

Reed keeps an eye on Laverne during the conversation without looking at her too directly or for too long. He hasn't mentioned his discovery to Dan – because perhaps this is another secret worth keeping and because he still has no way of explaining that Dan would understand.

'Now then,' Minnie says thoughtfully, rising to retrieve a small brown envelope from the dresser drawer.

She taps the corner of the envelope against the back of the settee as she thinks.

'Now what about extending the investigation – perhaps for a week? Up to you. We were rather hoping…'

'Well…' Dan says.

Reed thinks that Dan is probably just struggling to come up with a polite way of declining, but there is a small, anxious part of him that wonders if Dan is going to accept the extra work.

But we have found the necklace and it's right over there, he thinks, looking again at Laverne's scarf. This time, when she notices him looking, he doesn't look away.

Reed's eyes soften with kindness and Laverne offers a small, resigned smile.

Dan and Minnie notice them looking at one another, so Reed takes a slow breath, ready to speak.

'You're wearing it, aren't you?' he says, gently.

Minnie adopts a frown and looks from him to her sister. Then she moves toward Laverne and, ever so gently, touches the scarf. Laverne allows Minnie to move it aside. Her throat is bare: no necklace at all.

'But…'

Reed looks down at the carpet, with reddening cheeks.

Laverne, meanwhile, places her hand over Minnie's, which has come to rest, with the scarf, on her shoulder. She taps her sister's hand reassuringly and looks up at her.

'I was.' She nods. 'I *have* been wearing it, Minnie. Yes, it was me.'

Minnie looks into her eyes.

'Not for a séance or anything *like* that. I wouldn't want you to think…'

Minnie shakes her head ever so slightly, and strokes her sister's hair.

'I just wear it to feel close to her. Honestly, Minnie, that's all. Every now and then… it makes me feel better when I'm missing her, that's all.'

Dan tries to exchange a sheepish 'shall-we-get-out-of-here?' look with Reed but instead finds his friend transfixed by the scene, his expression burdened with worry. He looks like he regrets revealing something he shouldn't have and causing a painful rift.

'But why would you need to hide it from me?' Minnie asks.

Laverne joins her behind the settee.

'Oh, Minnie, I know how much it pains you to see it so…'

'No, no, you wear it whenever you want.'

They enfold one another in a hug.

This time, when Dan shoots a side glance at Reed, he finds his friend watching the sisters with moist, glistening eyes.

Dan taps a finger silently on the plump leather arm of his chair, waiting for the right moment to ask his question. The sisters hug a while longer and Reed blinks his way back to normal.

'So, where is it?' Dan asks.

***

Down in the office, Dan turns the dial of the safe in sequence of the secret code he set. As he opens the door, light angles inside, revealing the shining necklace. He picks it up and holds it for all to see. The hummingbird and the flowers rock gently between his hands.

'So...?'

Reed laughs. He doesn't understand it either, but it amuses him to watch Dan puzzling over the mystery. Dan pokes his head inside the safe to knock on its solid-sounding walls, then backs out again and aims a confused scowl at the sisters.

'How did you...?'

Laverne smiles and leans closer to her sister, cupping a hand to her ear. She whispers to Minnie and they smile.

'Magic!' Laverne says, finally answering Dan's question.

The sisters laugh warmly, catching the twinkle in one another's eye.

'No, come on, no – really?' Dan asks. 'Do *you* know?'

Reed's eyes widen and he folds his arms and shakes his head.

'Well…' Laverne begins.

Minnie touches her on the arm.

'No, no, let him have his puzzle. Now, Dan. You're an intelligent man. You'll be able to work it out.'

***

Back in the van outside, Dan and Reed sit motionless and confused, each watching Popplewell's Rare Books across the road.

Dan's darting, narrow eyes make him look as if he's trying to compute invisible maths problems, whereas Reed is altogether more adrift in his own little world. They have decided to leave the drive home until tomorrow and return to the hotel, but so far haven't even left the row of shops.

After another minute's thinking and silence, Reed draws a breath.

'I never knew that objects could have so much power.'

Dan waits a beat.

'You know that it wasn't really a magically *vanishing* necklace, don't you?'

'Yes, but I mean – the memories that thing holds for them, the emotions… you know.'

Reed's possessions consist only of a few practical items: his van, a selection of charity shop shirts, whatever paperback he is reading at the time… Though there was that small, tan cowboy hat – he had carried that around for years.

He adds something under his breath.

'Half the time I feel like *I'm* not even really here…'

Living a life half in the dreaming has given him a strange relationship to physical reality. What's important to Reed is whatever, in that moment, he is grasping in his hand.

Dan grunts, not really paying attention.

When Reed eventually looks at him, he sees Dan's expression; pained and grumpy.

'And what's up with you?'

'Man! I hate not knowing!'

***

This time, when Zoya walks into the school hall and hands over her cassette, she is determined to use her first choice.

'Side A,' she instructs the man. 'It's ready to go.'

As she greets the panel again, she sees that there are four people instead of three. All her determination almost falls to her feet as she realises that the extra person is Leon Foster himself. She feels nervous and insecure all over again.

She masks this by walking back to the centre spot, ruffling her loose curls.

She waits for the music to begin, making sure not to stare at Leon Foster, keeping herself agile on the balls of her feet.

She waits. The white noise portion of the tape stretches on too long.

She starts to wonder what she can possibly do with her dancing that she hasn't already shown them before. It was better when the panel were people she had never heard of.

It's okay, she tells herself again, *I'm the amateur, it's fine*, but then she remembers watching Leon Foster in the local theatre the other day; making movements so entrancing that they seemed to float like golden memories around the stage.

Zoya ruffles her hair again. When the guitars kick in, she has never felt *less* ready to start – but, as the music takes hold of her, she cannot do anything *but* dance.

***

Reed is walking through the streets on his way to get dinner from the chippy. He thinks he knows where he's going. Walking past a Victorian school building, he recognises a car by the kerb and follows his curiosity through the gates.

It *is* Zoya's Suzuki. This must be where her audition is. He spots an open door and wanders over to see what he can see. Maybe Zoya will want to join them for a fish supper when she's finished. Maybe he should go inside to wait.

Inside the school building, all is quiet; nobody is around. Perhaps it is the emptiness that makes him feel perfectly at home. Without particularly deciding to, he wanders through the hall until he hears faintly growing music and follows the sound around a corner.

As he advances along the unlit corridor, he recognises the tune as 'Dress' by PJ Harvey, one of Zoya's favourites. He moves toward the sound of the driving guitars and the wailing lyrics that conjure a scene.

In the shadows, he approaches a closed door and looks through the small square of safety glass into the hall.

Inside, he sees Zoya in the flow of dance. He sees her hair flashing through the space, and he sees her moving the way that only *she* moves. She seems to fly around the room, pulling his attention wherever she goes, like a rainbow trail.

Reed has seen Zoya dancing before. It made him fall in love with her.

He stands in the semi-darkness, watching, and nobody knows that he's there. He watches and his plans fall away to nothing.

All that she is doing is dancing to a song in a room — but it's the *way* she's doing it, painting the space with the very colours of her soul. So, it's true then, he realises with a sinking feeling; she still exists when she's not with *him*.

He finds himself backing away again, into the dark corridor and out into the night.

*****

After the audition and the thank-yous, Zoya sees the panel gathering their papers and unplugging the cassette player from the wall. As there's nobody auditioning after her, she takes a minute to towel off and wriggle into a sweater. She hears light footsteps approaching, and turns, expecting the return of her tape.

Leon Foster is standing there, holding it in his hand.

'Hi, I'm Leon,' he says, just like she doesn't know *exactly* who he is.

'I... I'm Zoya.'

She doesn't know if she should be shaking his hand or not, but the idea of touching her palm to his seems too much. His blond hair and blue eyes seem too colourful, like a theatre poster come to life. She manages to take the cassette from him and drop it into her bag.

She had shaken her nerves during the dancing, but now they are shooting back. *Never meet your heroes*, they say. She is thinking about the phrase. *Scared* is what she feels, then – scared that he will do or say something that shows he isn't the person she thinks he is. She'd prefer to cling on to the fantasy that he is basically the same person as her.

Then she realises that he's talking.

'Hey, I loved that thing you did.'

He illustrates the comment with a sketched movement of something she must have done during the audition.

'Really?'

'Oh, yeah, and how it was sort of...'

Instead of words, he uses his body, showing her a more realised version of what he did before.

'How was it?' he asks, thinking, wanting to get it just right.

'Oh, you mean this?'

Zoya recreates the move she remembers, a rolling, flowing thing that drops from shoulder to toe.

'Yeah. Hey, what about if you… if you sort of turned your hips at this point, do you mind if…?'

He gently touches her hip to indicate that she copy him – and that's what she finds herself doing; letting him improve the movement, mirroring what he does.

Zoya feels warm inside from the compliment and the impromptu lesson and the lightest of touches on her hip. She has seen that same hand carving out emotions up there on a spotlit stage. No wonder it felt electric, those fingertips lightly grazing her side.

'Yeah,' she says, 'that's… yeah… Thanks!'

Leon Foster looks around.

'They're waiting for me. Thanks, Zoya. Thanks for coming in. I enjoyed your audition.'

He walks away to join the huddle.

'Yeah, me too.'

She glides out of the hall, walking on air, the electrifying tingle warming her from head to toe.

***

Later, somewhere on the streets of the town, it is only when Reed accidentally stumbles upon a fish and chip shop that he even remembers what he went out to do.

C H A P T E R   9

On the road between Axworth and Kembleton, Reed sees Zoya's Suzuki in the wing mirror. She is flashing her lights.

'Is she stalking us or are we stalking her?' Dan jokes.

Zoya pulls alongside the van, pointing her finger at them before hooking it into a *follow me* sign. The two men nod and let her car tuck in on the road ahead.

'Did she seem happy?' Dan asks. 'I wonder how her audition went.'

***

A short drive later, the convoy pulls up outside Whale House. As they approach, sunlight bounces from one asymmetric window to the next, like stepping-stones – from kitchen to parlour to Abigail's room to Zoya's telescope turret at the top.

Reed can't help looking up to that window; to the sill where she clung on for her life; to the ridge where she found her footing and climbed back in. He looks there every time, perhaps because he has only heard about the events that night, perhaps because he can't shake the image of a different outcome: of Zoya falling, screaming, to her death.

Waiting for Zoya to get her things together and step out of her car, Reed leans against his camper van and looks at the house. The scents of drowsy summer drift up on air currents to the whale sculpture on the roof. Sometimes it seems to be mid swim. Today, somehow, it looks like it is napping.

He turns and looks over the town and to the sea. So much seemed to happen here over such a short time. He can never get over how small Shilly-on-Sea is, really, or how familiar the waves.

You can't always taste salt on the air up here, but today he can. Behind the house, the birch wood rustles with a whirling song. This strange old house – always different, always the same.

He hears Zoya's car door slam shut and turns around.

'Aren't you coming in?' she asks, as Dan insists on taking her bag.

They tread the path through the front garden to the door. The serrated leaves of the rose bushes paw at them as they pass. The blooms bake in the sunshine, turning technicolour like the old family photo albums he's been shown; Zoya, a young girl, already smiling and in love with the world.

As they walk, the door is opened from within. Richard and Abigail are waiting in the hall with spreading smiles.

'Someone's had a phone call,' Richard announces, unable to wait much longer.

As she gets closer, Zoya sees that his eyes are twinkling.

'The New Movement School?'

They all go inside.

'It's good news, honey,' Aunt Abigail says, squeezing Zoya's arm.

Zoya starts shaking her head.

'They're probably just calling to give me a polite rejection…'

'Oh no!' Richard says. 'Abigail wheedled it out of them – it's a definite yes!'

Zoya stands open-mouthed.

'Here's the message,' Aunt Abigail adds, pushing a piece of paper into Zoya's palm.

Zoya studies it and swallows and then looks from one face to the next. Then she dashes to the nearest phone, which is through in the garden room. She dials the number as everyone gathers just beyond the door – everyone but Richard, who has wheeled himself off into the kitchen to open the fridge. The others are making an unconvincing show of giving her some privacy.

Zoya half sits, half kneels sideways on an armchair, needlessly hunching over the telephone.

'Hello? Yes, this is Zoya Carmichael. You left a message with… Really?… I've got a place?… Yes… Yes, I'd love to accept… Yes, you can send it to the address on my form. Thanks! Yes… Yes, I can do that. Thanks again!'

She puts the receiver down and looks at it for a while.

'I told you!'

Aunt Abigail's warm voice breaks the tension.

'So,' Richard says, wheeling into the doorway, a chilled bottle in one hand. 'Is it also a yes from you?'

Zoya nods.

Richard pops the champagne cork while Abigail rushes around handing out glasses and Dan gathers Zoya up in a hug.

Having charged everyone else's glasses, Richard fills his own. The bubbles rise with a simmering fizz.

'To Zoya,' he says, leading the toast.

'I haven't done anything yet, Dad,' she protests.

'Yes, you have.' He regards her with an all-knowing gaze, then raises his glass once more. 'To taking a leap,' he says, and everybody toasts.

***

Sharon hangs up the payphone and bites her lip, thinking. A passing car makes her look up sharply and then she hurries along the pavement and back to the house. The drive is still empty, so she goes straight in.

'Alex?' she calls, waiting a moment for a reply.

Then she goes straight to the bedroom, stands on the bed, and drags a holdall from the mess shoved on top of the wardrobe.

She works quickly, packing just a few clothes and essentials, stopping dead now and then to listen for the door. The house is silent.

She zips up the bag and puts on a second jacket before closing the wardrobe and drawers. She smooths over the duvet where she had stood on it, her fingers slowing to a small, sad caress.

Then she leaves the bedroom and makes her way through the kitchen to the back door. In the laundry room, she pauses with her hand on the door handle.

Her eyes swivel to the tumble dryer, knowing what is hidden there. She bites her lip.

Quickly, she stoops to open the dryer door and squeeze out the leather bag. It hangs heavy in her grasp.

Outside, she slips through the gap in the hedge and heads toward the edge of the scrub. She reaches the brick wall and drops the bags down into the alley. Then, she plants her trainers solidly on top of the wall and takes the leap.

***

By the time the sun has shifted in the sky, Reed and Zoya are standing by his van.

The pages of the day have turned now, and the hill is lit with different colours. The pop-up picture book that is the town below is now edged with softer shadows and the distant bay finds a whole new shade, somewhere between postcard blue and documentary grey. The air is no longer salt sweet.

He hands Dan's overnight bag to Zoya.

'Thanks,' she says, taking the handle with both hands. 'You sure you didn't want to stay for dinner too? You know they love having people round.'

Reed shakes his head, looking in the vague direction of the coast road and the sea.

'You didn't need to come out and see me off,' he says.

Zoya flexes her shoulders a little and gives a small smile.

'Wanted to make sure I leave the premises, eh?'

She laughs and shakes her head. It's more of a reaction to his lame joke than an answer.

'So, have you got more paranormal cases on the books?' she asks.

Reed pulls a nonchalantly humble little face.

'Let me guess,' Zoya says, 'a 'Zwiffle'?'

He smiles, but it soon fades.

'So, I won't see you before you move to Falconshire.'

'No.'

'You'll be the star pupil in no time,' Reed says, reaching for something positive to say.

She wrinkles her nose in bemused disagreement.

'I think I'll just aim for fitting in.'

Reed looks out over the town, and finds those tall old sycamores cresting the rooftops of The Glebe with almost luminescent greens. The sky looks to be promising a pink sunset and Reed would like to be alone by then – some place by the waves where he can watch it with the company of his imagination, rather than the reality of someone who will no longer hold his hand.

Sometimes he catches Dan transfixed by a sunset and he seems to have a tear in his eye.

'So,' Reed says, moving his feet, 'drive carefully.'

'It's *you* who's leaving,' she points out.

'Is it?'

They look at one another as seconds drift past. Reed breaks away and heads toward his van.

'Right, I'll let you go,' he says, opening the door.

'Reed,' Zoya says, her voice making it sound important.

He pauses and turns to her.

'Make sure you spend more time with other humans, won't you?'

SEPTEMBER

CHAPTER 10

Zoya slows her Suzuki and narrows her eyes at the route ahead. By the time she reaches the give way line, she barely has to brake. She looks around at the country roads, turning her head this way then that. The sun-dappled, tree-lined lanes and rural vistas look pretty much the same in both directions, echoing the picture in her rear-view mirror. There are no cars on the roads and not a soul to ask.

She peers at the thick hedgerow opposite the junction, looking for a signpost, but, if there ever *was* one, it has been swallowed by wild, verdant, summer growth.

The engine ticks over. The waving canopy is shading and revealing the road with sunlit pockets of lime and gold. Dappled pools of light dance on leaves at the roadside, fluttering papery patterns of hearts, daggers and sails.

She reaches to the passenger seat to unearth the New Movement School information pack and check the written directions. If she is where she thinks she is, she should be taking a right.

She trusts her instinct, drops the handbrake and makes the right turn.

***

Ten minutes later and she is doubting herself and wondering whether to fish the *A–Z* out of the boot. These quiet ribbons of rural highway make for a pleasant drive, but she feels she should be there by now. The rolling scenery is starting to look the same, as if turned by stagehands while her wheels run rollers and she stays exactly where she is. Sometimes Reed's surreal sense of humour works its way into her head. She shakes the notion out of her mind. She focusses on the sunny, shadowy road ahead. Surely, she will notice the gate.

The easy hum of the engine is matched by the sound of trees whirling in light applause. The passing car provokes plump wood pigeons to flapping, cracking flight.

In some places, the deep, dark undergrowth is teeming with feathered leaves and fronds like octopus arms. In other, sunnier, places, bushy grasses lean into the baked, unmarked lanes, waving tiny flowers like distant stars.

She has seen a picture of the dance school – surprisingly modernist in architectural style but certainly noticeable; confidently poised amid sweeping, grassy grounds.

The lane curves gently left and right.

A strolling grouse panics and takes flight, gliding over a hedge and into a field. Around another bend, dandelion parachutes scatter like soap bubbles; tiny feathered seeds dancing a delicate ballet in the air.

She makes out a gap in the hedgerows and slows the car to a stop, looking for a sign. She wonders why she hasn't encountered any other new arrivals on the roads. Is everybody else here ahead of her? Have they all registered and moved in already? Is she late?

There *is* something hidden in the trees: an old wooden signpost revealed when the broad, flapping leaves are part-ed by the slow, lazy breeze. She can't read all of the faded, shallow letters but it's enough for her to turn off the lane and through the gate.

Emerging from the tree cover, Zoya enters the grounds. Her Suzuki progresses up a drive that runs along the edge of a gnarly wood, tyres turning over fine-grained gravel the colour of a beach.

The wood falls away behind a cluster of buildings and she finds herself in the black-and-white photograph from the brochure – only, the *real* dance school in front of her is shining and glinting in the sun. She sees the main entrance. This must be the place.

The school stands, modestly grand, at the top of the rise. Brick and wood and glass meet in angles and sharp-cut corners, rooted to the drive by shallow, inviting steps.

Below the hall sweeps an expanse of sea-green grass-es, thick enough to sink your feet into, spiky with fingery fronds and bobbing with daisies. A wheeling pair of white butterflies weave around one another to the distant reaches of the field; tiny yachts in a wide bay.

A sudden, rippling breeze zips across the grounds to-ward her open window. It smells of the countryside and nothing of the sea.

She idles a moment, looking at the building ahead of her. Through the windowed wall, she can just about make out the iconic staircase although the interior is camouflaged by waves of leafy, sun-dappled reflections that dance across the glass.

She looks around the site again, spotting some kind of outdoor stage down the slope to the right and other unidentified outbuildings almost at the distant perimeter. She makes out tall trees at the far side, their branches waving a patient *hello*.

Then someone walks around the corner and sets an A-frame on the ground.

Welcome Dancers! Parking this way, it reads, illustrated with an arrow.

The lean young man who placed it looks up and sees Zoya watching. He beckons her along and smiles.

OCTOBER

CHAPTER 11

Zoya and the others are in Studio 1. Striped maple floorboards flex with the gentle thud of feet. The mirror that stretches from wall to wall is filled with a reflection of wood panelling, moving bodies and green, window-framed trees.

It's the end of class and the dancers are a bit giddy – more from the hit-and-miss nature of the move they are trying out than from the twisting and spinning it requires. Someone's foot squeaks against the floor.

'That's right, Sharon, you don't step out of it until the last moment,' the teacher, Mya, is saying, pacing the room.

A strip of high, open windows allows the cooling breath of nature to make fresh forays into the sweat-warm studio, but no birdsong or whistling breezes can be heard over all the encouraging instruction and little grunts of effort bouncing around the room. Everyone is trying to put into practice what they have been taught.

'Yes, Olivia! You're getting it. Remember, everyone – soft knees. You can come out of it very low and still right yourself if you remember to keep soft knees. It won't hurt. Braver, Jo, you need to be braver with it. Think of a runner, right? Runners don't have contact with the ground at all times – and if they did, they couldn't run.'

The studio rings with the slap of feet, the chatter of students and the snap of elasticated waistbands being adjusted.

'Beautiful, Zoya! Fearless! Now, try to achieve that moment of suspension as you transfer your weight into it.'

Zoya stops and runs the back of her hand across her sweaty brow.

'Like this,' Leon Foster adds softly.

He is weaving among the dancers toward the back of the room, but when he models the start of the move, it is just for her. She tries it that way and he winks at her before moving along.

'Okay! Dancers!' Mya calls in her wrapping-up-the-lesson voice. 'That's the end of class. Stretch it out now. You know the score, stretch it out. And five, six, seven, eight...'

*****

By the bags, Zoya finds herself next to Leon Foster, who is towelling off. There's something she's been wanting to say to him for the past few weeks. She sneaks a glance at the purple T-shirt falling from his shoulder, and he sees her looking, so now she *has* to say it.

'I loved that show,' she says, looking more obviously at the *Liberte!* logo across his chest.

She saw him in that show on the West End – years ago now, but she still remembers.

He smiles at her, his face crinkling around those bright, blue eyes. In one swift motion, he lifts the T-shirt, wriggling his muscular back out of it, and gently throws it at her. She catches it in a clasp against her chest.

'Here. Have it.'

It feels soft and slightly damp in her hands, her fingers already tangling with the fabric.

'Sorry about the sweat.'

He smiles as he walks off and is practically gone before she can say thanks.

As everyone towels off, drinks water, changes into fresh clothes and gathers their bags, Zoya finds herself tarrying slightly. As the last of the group, Sandy and Lauren, leave the studio, Zoya stoops to re-tie the lace of a trainer that doesn't really need re-tying.

Alone in the studio, she quickly changes out of her T-shirt and into his.

***

Turning the corner from the modernist block to the residential wing, she sees a small commotion in the distance. At the other end of the shiny corridor, Luke Boyd seems to have dropped some bags. Luke is the first person she met here – the man with the welcome sign. He is the office administrator and a generally do-anything-for-you, helpful kind of chap.

As she draws nearer, she sees him, back to her, scrabbling to gather the things. She sees cash scattered all over the floor. A lot of it. More than anyone should keep about their person anyway. So much that it would feel weird to help Luke tidy it up.

Zoya finds herself pausing by the noticeboard as if checking on her timetable. Out of the corner of her eye, she sees Luke gathering the notes back into a leather bag and then scooping up the rest of the luggage and disappearing from view.

She fills her bottle from the water fountain, leaving a polite pause before heading around the corner to the stairs. As she walks up to her floor, her calves feel a little tight. Maybe she hasn't stretched enough.

As she approaches her bedroom door, she sees that it is ajar. A man's voice is coming from inside.

'... happy to help. Listen, I don't want to pry, but have you got a bank account set up yet? It's just that it's a lot safer than keeping money in your room… Come into Rithling on the coach, Friday. I'll help you get one set up…'

'I will, thanks.'

Luke backs out of the room, almost bumping into Zoya. Inside, she sees Sharon sitting on the other bed, her bags dumped on the mattress around her.

'I almost forgot!' Zoya says.

'It's still okay, isn't it?' Sharon asks.

'Of course!'

'I'll leave you ladies to it,' Luke says, rolling his fingers in a light scale on the door frame; one task down, a hundred to go. He paces off and down the stairs. Zoya closes the door and sits on her own bed.

'He was helping me move rooms. You *don't* mind sharing, do you?'

'Not at all.'

'I just... didn't really feel... comfortable on the ground floor...'

'That's alright. I like company. Everyone else shares...'

'Well, thanks.'

As Zoya collects her shower things, she notices Sharon zipping up the leather bag tightly, and pushing it deep under her new bed.

***

Tonight, I am exploring. I have come as far as Rithling, the local market town down the road. It has taken me a while to walk here, but I managed not to get lost in the leafy lanes.

I made my way to the town centre, hoping to beat my alarm clock and find somewhere high enough for falling. All roads seem to spill out into the town square, which is where a few taller buildings stand. In the half of the square not given over to a car park, a handful of curled ochre-coloured leaves drop windlessly, from a tree planted in the paving, and come to a rustling, shrivelled stop by the trunk. I look around, trying to assess the climbing potential of the pub, the bank, the parade of shops...

The coming dawn is brightening the square; so much that I can read the time on the town hall clock. I've got less than thirty minutes until I have to wake up for class.

The town hall itself isn't as high as I'd ideally like and it looks like the climb might take a while.

I spin around and assess the police station, which stands at the other side of the square, beyond the low-walled car park. It isn't really high enough either, but there is a useful looking fire escape at the side.

It will have to do. I jog across and start scaling the metal stairs.

At the top, I carry on climbing. I grip the guttering, one foot on the railing as my other scrabbles against the wall. I make it onto the flat roof.

I still have a good fifteen minutes before my alarm will wrench me from the dreaming. I take a minute to look around.

The subtle sunrise is developing like a photograph; baby blues emerging from the grey without fanfare, a splash of frosted peach indicating the direction of the still-submerged sun. As the colour palette dials itself to daylight, I notice cool, distant grasses scenting the sky. I look up and see a fine breath of high fog curling around the hilltops. The sun is about to come up.

The slopes across the river look lime and crimson in the strange morning light. I decide to go toward them as there is more of a drop behind the building at that side.

First, I place my feet on the edge of the rooftop and then I make two long, deliberate strides back. I focus on the spot and count myself in.

… five, six, seven, eight…

Then I rush to the edge, lift to my toes and twist into the controlled drop. I feel it: a moment of impossible suspension before the flying fall.

***

The impact sprays dust particles up from the ground; the thump of shoulders against concrete, followed by a whimper. Darren is on the floor, trying not to cry.

Urgent footsteps rush toward him at head level, out of the door light and into the dark.

'Then who *did* take it, Darren?'

Darren feels his face sticky. His head throbs and some part of it is stinging with blood and dirt. He watches Alex's boots in the darkness, tensing for the kick. He raises a hand with some effort.

'I… don't know!' he shouts. 'I don't know, Alex! Mick Staines hasn't been seen since…'

The suggestion stops Alex for a moment, giving him pause to think. Then, he steps over Darren and walks off into the night.

Darren hears the Capri speed off and stays down, shivering and bleeding on the floor.

'It wasn't *that* bad a beating, was it?' says one of the bouncers, Jeff.

They have been watching from inside the gaping fire exit. Light spills from the club, giving the yard an amber sheen. A wall of fuzzy, muffled music masses behind them. They look at each other.

'Not dead, is he?'

Pete shakes his head and goes out into the yard. He stoops to touch Darren's arm.

'Come on, Daz, get up now. *We'll* have to clean up this mess.'

'A minute. Leave me a minute,' Darren pleads, rolling slightly on the floor.

Pete stands up again and looks at Jeff in the corridor light. They wait a while, standing awkwardly, starting to feel embarrassed for him. Darren rolls onto his knees and cradles his head.

'Full of surprises – Alex,' Pete says, re-joining Jeff at the open doorway, where they almost block the light.

'His woman left.'

'Sharon? No!'

Darren has gotten himself to a kneeling position; droplets of blood seem to fall from his face, catching in the light and splattering quietly on the stone.

'You're alright, Daz. Come on, we'll get you up and clean you off,' Jeff says.

They wander back toward his spot on the floor.

'I never realised Alex had such a soft heart,' Pete says as the two bouncers each take an arm.

Darren hangs limply between them. They continue talking over his head. Jeff gets his first look at the state of him in the light.

'Jesus,' he says, addressing Pete. 'Note to self: never steal from Alex Belasis.'

Pete nods slowly before adding: 'And never break his heart.'

They ease Darren up onto his feet and lead him back inside the club.

CHAPTER 12

Zoya wakes with a headache. Daylight stings the back of her eyes. She raises her palms to her forehead instinctively and softly strokes her skull.

There is a wet patch of dribble on her pillow and the twisting marshmallow duvet seems to be swallowing her up. The brightly coloured bedding she brought from home doesn't really go with the room, but it's still a better option than the bland, peach version provided by the dance school that Sharon is making do with.

She can see by the light of the tall window between their beds that Sharon is up and about. They had soon agreed to get rid of the net curtains and open up the view. She watches the silent trees. A conversation passes by in the corridor and a hot water pipe is knocking somewhere.

Sweet scents spill from the bathroom and Sharon's wardrobe is softly opened and closed. Her feet rub against the wiry carpet.

'You look like you were wasted last night,' Sharon says, noticing that Zoya is awake.

Sharon is getting organised for the day, already dressed.

'I haven't been drinking. Not even a little bit,' Zoya says, propping herself up in the bed.

She stares out of the window; nothing but the distant trees.

Sharon emerges from the bathroom again, this time with her fine fair hair pulled back in a ponytail. She's wearing dance gear, like they all always do.

'Bathroom's all yours,' she says brightly. 'See you at breakfast.'

Zoya, who had been ruffling her hair until it curtained her eyes from the daylight, stops and parts it with a breath. She looks at the alarm clock. She's not late yet but will need to get a move on. She jerks to a sitting position, legs on the carpet, and then hunches over, her hands gripping the edge of the bed, curls tickling her knees.

Why does she feel so rough?

Remembering the power of deep breaths, she re-oxygenates herself, slowly getting the churning under control. She puts it down to a poor night's sleep. Maybe.

Then, she hops off the bed and flits to the wardrobe, committed to tackling the day ahead.

***

An hour or so later, Zoya is sitting in the canteen among the dregs of breakfast and the whole class. She found a spare seat at the table with Sandy, Tilda and Lauren and is glugging deep draughts from her water bottle in between the chat.

Tilda is talking about some money missing from her bank that she can't account for. The combination of ditzy and well-off could make Tilda extremely annoying, but

Zoya is already so fond of her – and of everyone – that, somehow, it's not.

The chatter filling the atrium subtly changes in tone as meeting time draws near. People wind up their conversations, one eye on the staircase where the directors usually appear.

Meredith Lucas stands up from the table where she has been eating with some of the dancers and approaches the bottom of the modernist stairs. Her fringe is as straight and perfect as always and her expression as kind. Zoya can't help admiring the geometric patterned garment she is wearing. Not everyone could carry it off.

Jerrod Harrington often appears for the meetings from the direction of the offices upstairs. Zoya strongly suspects he just likes to make a dramatic entrance – descending the iconic staircase while everyone looks.

Here he comes now. She can see him reflected in the plate glass. He still has a dancer's physique and always dresses in black. When she first saw the pair of them on the first day, matching in their monochrome, artsy way, the directors had seemed a bit much, but now they've grown on her. At least, Meredith has.

Meredith is now leaning by the bannister, chatting to Olivia and Clare who happen to be sitting nearby. Soon, everyone turns themselves to face the stairs.

It makes sense to have the meetings now – when everyone is in the same place and too full of food to dance. The joke name for these meetings is 'the daily digest' – a name probably invented by a previous cohort many years ago, but that now feels, very much, *theirs*.

Zoya still finds it hard to picture any other group of dancers here, or a time when Sandy, Tilda, Lauren, Jo, Clare, Ivan, Olivia… and everyone have been swept away into the past.

Usually, the daily digest is a short meeting – a mix of timetable information and pep talk, but sometimes it leads to longer discussions; all part of the collaborative ethos of the school – or 'project', she thinks, correcting herself. That's what they like to call it here.

Meredith and Jerrod are now standing by the bannister, waiting for hush.

From her position at the edge of the room, Zoya can see Luke, the administrator, dismounting his high-spec bike outside. Zoya has noticed him before, escaping into the dewy morning air, taking off for a long ride before work. Cycling seems to be his thing.

She imagines it makes him feel the way that she feels in the full flow of dance.

'So, today's meeting will be quite a short one,' Jerrod says, finally commanding everyone's attention. 'There are just a couple of things on the agenda.'

'That's right,' Meredith adds. 'So, the first thing to say is – well done, everyone. You've worked really hard so far – it's been a wonderful first month. And… you know, we really try to pick people who will be the best fit for the group but who will also be able to bring something of *themselves* to the experience too' – she looks with dancing eyes at Jerrod – 'and, you know, we really think that, with your group, we've achieved it.' She clasps her hands to her lips, almost in prayer pose, and then points her fingertips out to the room of listening students. '*You've* achieved it.'

Everyone takes in her sentiment, glancing at one another, nodding, smiling. It doesn't feel cheesy because they already feel like a group of friends working together, sharing something special. And out here, in the wooded grounds – where even Rithling is starting to feel like the big smoke – there is *only* progress and friendship and dance.

'So, thank you everyone,' adds Jerrod, keen to share the focus and rising a step. 'Now, the second thing is that, from now on, we're all going to be working on the Valentine Show.'

Excitement swings through the room.

'Relax,' Lauren says, noticing Zoya rolling her eyes. 'They only call it that because of the time of year, it isn't all pas de deux and romance.'

They share an amused smile.

'In February, we'll be staging a show in Kedbury,' Meredith adds, taking the mantle. 'It's becoming a tradition and we usually get quite a good crowd. And, please, invite all your family and friends along too.'

Zoya wonders if the date clashes with Richard and Abigail's cruise.

'But you're going to have to work even harder from now on,' Meredith continues, sweeping the room with a happy intense gaze, 'because *you're* going to be choreographing it!'

'With our help, of course,' Jerrod says, 'and with Mya and Leon's,' he adds, picking out the latter at a table across the room.

Leon, who barely looks up from reading a copy of *The Dancer* magazine, gives a bouncy, stagey wave.

'So, that's going to be the focus of our classes from now on,' Jerrod is saying. 'We're going to develop you not only as dancers, but as *choreographers*.'

'I know you're all capable of what we're asking of you and we're really excited to get started,' Meredith says.

'So, that's what we're doing after breakfast,' Jerrod adds, unnecessarily, before busting out the call and response that still makes Zoya cringe.

'Remember,' he says, 'We're a *team* because…'

'Together Everyone Achieves More!'

***

Later, after the morning class, Zoya looks up to see Leon walking toward her across the maple floor.

'So, what did you make of the capoeira class? I knew you'd be a natural.'

Zoya's self-conscious diffidence cannot override her happy smile.

'Hey, I thought of something for you,' Leon continues, full of excitement.

He begins to model a new move for her: just like that.

'Come on, try it with me, you step-wide and keep rolling it to the toe, then drop with the other knee and – yes! – I knew it would suit you… Hey, I'm loving your arm there – really let it go!'

'Is that not what you meant…?'

'No, it's awesome! Come on, rag-dolly, let's go to lunch.'

He steps his feet together and curves his arm into a neat crook. She grins again, linking her arm with his as they file out of the studio.

***

'Just us, then?'

Toby Prosser is leaning toward the passenger door of the minibus addressing Sandy and Tilda on the tarmac.

The friends give final assurances that they are staying on in Rithling for a bit and will make their own way back, before waving to Toby and Zoya on the coach and heading across the square.

Toby buckles his belt and starts the engine before looking around to Zoya, who is sitting alone a few seats behind; evidently, they are having the same thought.

She moves up to the first seat by the driver, smiling.

'Hi,' he says.

'Hi.'

The minibus is so familiar to her now: the striped fabric of the seats; the way the carpeting runs right up to the line of windows like man-made moss; reassuring, like a landscape mapped. She feels happy listening to the comforting rattle and hum of the engine, the rasping grip of the tyres.

The vehicle wends its way out of the town centre and toward the quiet lanes, the pair of them chit-chatting as they go.

'So, what *did* bring you to work at the dance school?' Zoya asks, after a pause. 'There must be lots of accountancy-financey jobs at less out-of-the-way places?'

'Accountancy-financey-*drivery* jobs?' he says, grinning, 'Nah – it's a winning and unique combination.'

She gives a laughing little breath.

'Actually,' he continues, 'I wasn't brought here – I was brought *back.*'

Zoya's expression, when he looks at her, shows that she would like to hear more.

'Yeah, I grew up around here and, well, my mother still lives up on the tops.'

Zoya senses something he isn't saying out loud.

'Is she... okay?'

He swallows, concentrating on the road ahead.

'Physically, yes. Mentally...? She's suffering with dementia.'

He looks at her and pulls a stoic, fact-of-life expression.

'Although, looking at it from the other side of the river, "suffering" might not be the word for it. She's happy most of the time – happier than most. She's living in her home, she has her things around her, she has friends who visit, I'm there...'

'That's good.'

Zoya still doesn't know what to make of Toby Prosser. She looks slyly at his sweater and unflattering glasses. He looks like the last person you'd expect to find at a progressive dance school but now, perhaps, she understands. He's always friendly but she doesn't know much about him... yet. Someone said he'd had a wife who'd died.

The brakes sigh.

'Looking at it from the other side of the river?' Zoya quotes. It's a phrase she doesn't know.

'Yeah, you know, like... the other side of the fence, it must be a local saying, I suppose – like "see things from a different point of view".'

Zoya nods.

'So, she's okay then, your mother?'

'It's just, you know, those moments of confusion that might frighten her. And I can't be there all the time. We've got carers going in to see her and it's not yet that advanced but... it just makes you worry.'

Zoya nods. She instantly feels for him. She never got the chance to care for her mother when she was dying of cancer, because she was only a little girl.

'Yeah, it must be hard.'

Zoya looks out of the window again, watching the bright layers of autumn countryside sliding by, her reflection gliding over the scenery like a ghost. She has a feeling that she is trying to decipher but can't quite put into words. All she got to do was take.

Then she remembers Aunt Abigail telling her something, in her inimitable 'Aunt Abigail' kind of way: *'You weren't put on this earth to serve people, honey, nobody was. Be kind, be considerate to others – but be your own person too.'*

Zoya smiles to herself again. The minibus rolls to a stop.

'Actually…' Toby begins.

She looks at him.

'Would you mind if we make a brief detour at Mum's? I just have some bits to drop off. Won't be a long visit; you can stay put on the bus.'

Zoya thinks of the one-to-one tuition she was hoping to get with Mya. That's the reason she was getting a lift back now. She glances at the time.

'Okay, my tuition isn't for a bit.'

Toby smiles and, at the junction, turns the minibus in the other, unfamiliar, direction.

'It's not far.'

***

Soon they are driving up a gently rising lane to an area that locals call 'the tops'. The trees grow more sparsely here and some of the wind-stripped branches are already losing their leaves.

As the crow flies, this area is quite close to the dance school but, somehow, it feels even more remote.

They pull up by a neat farmhouse that stands in a long strip of garden reaching from roadside to porch. Drying meadow grasses are turning autumnal hues, like a colour photograph fading in the sun. The cottage walls are seamed with thick stones at the corners and above the door. Zoya can't see Mrs Prosser at any of the windows.

Toby gathers a small bag together and makes to get out of the minibus.

'Won't be long – unless you want to come in and meet Mum?'

'Oh no, I'll just wait…' She uncrosses her legs and has a new thought. 'Actually, do you think she would mind if I nipped in, just to use the toilet?'

'Course not.'

They get out and walk up the path. She hears a chain of country whispers curving across the manured fields and fallow acres. Sepia grasses tickle her ankles as she nears the house.

Toby doesn't even lock the minibus door; no need to, out here in the sticks.

***

'And this is the peacock brooch I wore at my sister's wedding to Archie,' Mrs Prosser says, handing Zoya the brooch.

The keepsake trunk stands open on the floor by Mrs Prosser's feet where she can easily look through it all, gently handling each precious item as she tells Zoya all about it. Zoya kneels attentively on the carpet, genuinely interested in Mrs Prosser's things and life.

The living room is cosy with thick fleece rugs and blankets. A cardigan has been draped over the pillowy swell of Mrs Prosser's chair.

Zoya has stopped watching the clock now. She can hear the pleasant tapping of Toby's hammer as he fixes the stuck dresser upstairs.

'Was it a lovely wedding?' Zoya asks and is delighted that her question makes Mrs Prosser smile.

During the short space of their meeting, Zoya has learnt that factual questions seem to momentarily upset her but that taking an interest in her memories lights her up.

Mrs Prosser has a beautiful smile.

Zoya hands back the antique brooch and watches Toby's mother place it back in the trunk. The corners are graced by lavender-scented lace parcels to keep the contents smelling sweet. Mrs Prosser strokes the silk of her own wedding dress with her papery fingers for a moment, causing the interleaved tissue to rustle. Zoya watches her admiring the soft sheen of the material and texture of the hand-embroidered flowers. Perhaps she is filled with happy memories of that day, of her husband and their life together – or perhaps she is simply admiring the fabric in the afternoon light.

Zoya is enjoying the Ella Fitzgerald CD that Toby put on as soon as they came in, explaining in a low voice that music is a great way for people with dementia to reconnect with themselves. The gently ticking clock on the mantle warmly rings the quarter hour.

The soft tapping from upstairs only seems to add to the cosiness of her home. The kettle boils in the kitchen and Zoya gets up to go and make the teas.

When she returns to the sitting room, she finds it empty and worries. Quickly, she sets down the mugs and searches the downstairs rooms.

'Mrs Prosser? Marianne?'

Zoya calls her name a few times, but not loudly enough for Toby to hear. For some reason, she feels like she is somehow responsible for losing his mother, despite dismissing it as a stupid thing to think.

She sees the side door ajar and makes her way outside. Finding the long front garden empty, she ventures along the path and around the back. There is a cherry tree toward the rear of the back garden, and there she sees her: Mrs Prosser, lying beneath it on the grass.

Zoya runs over.

'Mrs Prosser! Are you alright?'

The panic ebbs from her voice when she sees her – lying quite happily in the swaying grasses and looking skywards with twinkling violet eyes.

Zoya kneels beside her, confused. She is beginning to wonder if Marianne has fallen into some kind of trance when she hears her saying something.

'Beautiful.'

Zoya nestles into the wild lawn besides her and follows her gaze.

The orange leaves of the cherry tree are fluttering on bouncing boughs above them, rustling like sliding waves, glowing like jewels in the light. Diamonds of sunshine trickle to the ground.

It *is* beautiful, Zoya thinks.

'Mrs Prosser, do you often lie on the ground like this?'

Marianne laughs.

'You know we do!'

Zoya wonders who Marianne thinks Zoya is right now, but it clearly doesn't matter to Marianne – and, lying there on the soft ground admiring the living painting above them, it doesn't matter to Zoya either.

'They say we should act with more decorum, now that we are grown up, but I say flapdoodle. Why should only children and men get to enjoy life?'

Her eyes are shining with sunlight, bright against the dappling shade. Zoya falls instantly in love with her. The women lie in parallel lines on the grassy bank letting the afternoon roll over them and the teas in the living room grow cold.

***

Zoya still carries that warm feeling when they pull into the driveway at the school and get out.

The drive home had been quiet and weird, though. Toby had reacted oddly to finding his mother and Zoya outside, and hardly spoke on the journey back.

Still, she agreed to help him carry the boxes of files up to the office because of-course-she-would. After some awkward box balancing by the wall and one-handed ferreting about in his pockets, Toby manages to pass Zoya the office key.

Stashing her own box under one arm, she gets the door unlocked and holds it open for Toby with her foot. She follows him in.

Zoya hasn't been in the admin office before and looks around.

'Should I put this one here?' she asks, setting her box down on top of a filing cabinet.

'Oh, yes, that's fine,' he says, moving the other boxes around on the desk.

'So, this is where the magic happens?' she asks.

He laughs. She likes the thaw in his mood.

He sinks into the desk chair.

'So, I have to ask,' she continues, 'what's in the boxes?'

'Oh, nothing. Files. They're just coming back from the audit. And that's the glamourous world of accountancy. And now, I've got to get all of the contents into those filing cabinets over there.'

He's keeping it friendly, but it is meant as a cue for her to leave.

'I'll help.'

Toby looks at her warily.

'Er… you're not really supposed to be in here…' he says, thinking her offer through.

He looks around at all the boxes and seems to reconsider.

'Okay then, thanks.'

***

By the time they get to emptying the last couple of boxes, Zoya has learnt that Toby can play the ukulele and that they both enjoy toasted teacakes and reruns of *Mission Impossible*.

She kneels to open a low filing cabinet drawer as the telephone rings and Toby edges around the desk to answer it. Beneath the thin, end-of-the-alphabet hanging files, she sees something in the bottom of the drawer. At first, she wonders if the long strip has become detached from something but, when she turns it over, she sees that there are thin electrical ribbons flattened against it.

It puzzles her, so she looks closer. She notices a tiny hole that makes her think of some kind of spy kit. She hears Toby wrapping up the phone call and decides not to ask about whatever it is. She puts it back – exactly as she found it – and closes the drawer.

'Thanks for your help today, Zoya. Can I interest you in an instant coffee for your troubles?'

'Oh. Thanks, but no. I have to go.'

***

Later, after street dance, Zoya is in the bathroom taking a shower. Something doesn't feel right.

She looks around at the fixtures and fittings, the tiles, the ceiling light. The water runs in comforting, hot sheets over her body and she blinks splashes from her eyes to see.

She turns the shower off and, as the rivulets fall from her skin, she suddenly feels more naked, more exposed.

She grabs up her towel, wrapping it around her body and clutching the corners to her neck with tight, balling fists.

She thinks of the unidentified strip in the filing cabinet and the tiny hole. A pinhole, she thinks, naming it, and immediately thinks of the word 'camera'. There *were* wires coming off it, she remembers. Shouldn't she just have asked Toby what it was, there and then?

With a jab, she wipes away condensation and looks at herself in the bathroom mirror, wondering why she is creeping herself out.

C H A P T E R 1 3

Zoya and Leon are standing and talking, just inside Studio 2.

'So, you got a solo piece!' Leon is saying. 'And how are you feeling about that?'

'Good,' she answers, 'good.'

It seems both exciting and daunting and she is still processing the programme that the directors just announced. Her mind is already awash with choreography ideas.

Mya walks in and swiftly sets up for her class.

'You'd better go,' Zoya says. 'You know, she's very…'

She pulls a face instead of a word.

'I know. Show you those lifts later on?' he says, checking on their arrangement before vacating the room.

Just then, the door swings open and Luke Boyd starts talking to Leon in the doorway.

'Zoya will do it. I've got a one-to-one now, in Studio 5.'

Zoya hears her name mentioned and looks toward them. Mya is calling out instructions at the front of the class now and is giving Zoya a pointed look. Zoya edges to the door.

'Do what?'

'Olivia Green needs a lift to the hospital. You know, her sister with the anorexia. She needs to go and see her, but Toby's out with the minibus.'

'What's happened? Is it an emergency?'

'No, no, I don't think so, just she promised and there's nobody to give her a lift.'

'Erm, can't she get a taxi? I don't want to miss my class…'

It seemed a perfectly reasonable response when she thought it, but, the way that Leon is looking at her, maybe it came out with the wrong tone. Luke is already running other options through in his mind. His fingers perform a light drum roll on the door he is holding open.

'Never mind. She's waiting for me in the office; we'll sort something out.'

He disappears again and Zoya re-joins the class. She had been looking forward to it, but now everything feels off.

Out of the corner of her eye, she watches Leon pad out of the studio and down the corridor. He doesn't look at her or wave his usual goodbye.

***

Sharon works the knife and the scone splits into two – just the right amount of crumbling. Having seen the size of them, they agreed to share. She drops her half onto a new plate and pushes the other across the table for Zoya.

'Thanks.'

They are in their favourite café in Rithling town square. The place is pleasantly busy and, when the kitchen door opens, there is a burst of culinary hiss and a glint of shining cookware that adds to the happy ambience. It brings the smell of sizzling bacon and something delicious being baked.

They set about buttering and jamming their scone halves, sipping their drinks and people-watching the town outside. They are sitting in a booth by a broad window, the pane edged with a hair's breadth of chill air.

'Exciting about the show, isn't it?' Sharon says as they watch the world go by.

'Yeah. Are you pleased with your allocation?'

Sharon smiles.

'I am. I think it will be really cool to see what we can do with the group, you know, the different ideas and combinations and shapes, I… Yeah, I'm excited about working with the others. Oh but' – she stops and shifts position – 'but you've got a solo, haven't you?'

The way Sharon says it indicates that she feels bad for Zoya having to work on her choreography alone, like she must be missing out.

'No, I'm pleased about it!'

'Oh. Right.'

Zoya watches a couple of pensioners walk past in the town square outside.

'Hey, can I ask you something?'

Sharon's expression seems to say: *fire away.*

'Do you have any family? Sorry, I just, you've never mentioned anyone, and I wondered if…'

Sharon cuts off Zoya's babbling with a kind and well-timed interjection.

'No, it's fine – you're right, I don't.'

She takes a healthy bite of the buttery, jammy scone.

'No, I didn't want to pry, I just thought… maybe I like the idea of doing a solo because, back home, I still live at home, with my dad, and my aunt too, now, and it's the town I grew up in and I see the same group of friends I've known since school and I work – or worked – in a café, with old friends and' – Zoya sits back and takes a breath – 'and I love all that, and all those people – and I love the whole group of us at NMS too but… I think I like the opportunity to strike out on my own.'

Sharon licks a smear of strawberry from her lips and looks at her with interest.

'I get it. But, you're right – it's different for me.'

Zoya nods, waiting to hear more about Sharon's so-far-mysterious background, but a question comes instead.

'So, what about your boyfriend?' Sharon asks, slurping from her mug, her hazel-green eyes shining with curiosity over the rim.

'I don't have a boyfriend,' Zoya answers, bemused.

Sharon looks a tiny bit puzzled.

'So, who's that guy you keep talking about? Er, "Rod"?'

'Oh no, that's… No, that's just a friend.'

Zoya hadn't been aware of even mentioning him, but she immediately knows who Sharon means.

'Were you living alone then?' Zoya asks.

Sharon purses her lips for a second, considering her answer, but, when it comes, it is a simple one.

'No, with an ex.'

It seems that that is the end of the story though because Sharon soon changes the topic.

'Hey, bet you regret not buying that trout jug from the Oxfam shop?'

Zoya laughs. They have been having lots of fun examining the random tat to be found in the local charity shops, particularly the ornaments: cutesy deer with big eyes; a frog sitting like a human; a clown with a puppy; the saddest bear you'll ever see.

'You should see the sculpture of a whale on top of my dad's house!' Zoya says, remembering that this isn't normal for a house.

Sharon laughs as much as Zoya thought she would, and Zoya edges a plastic charity shop bag onto the table, hoping this will go down as well.

'I got you this,' Zoya says, almost sheepishly, and pushes the gift across to her.

The tabletop has lost some of its shine, its surface now variegated with a pattern like ocean cartography. Zoya leaves the neatly folded bag in front of Sharon.

'It's not... Well, it really suited you.'

Zoya hopes this isn't coming across as charity, but untenses when she sees Sharon's warm smile. She accepts the present and squeezes Zoya's hand and they fall back easily into their conversation, trading observations about sleepy south-west villages and gritty north-east towns.

Soon, they slip into a game, inventing lives and silly secrets for the people they watch walking past; their own real-life stories blurring with the imagined ones of passers-by.

'Hey, there's Ivan and Jo!' Sharon exclaims.

Zoya sees them crossing the distant corner of the square and heading into the Rithling Arms.

'We said we'd join them?' Sharon prompts, gathering her shopping.

Zoya starts putting her jacket on.

'Let's do it!'

***

The next day, after modern jazz class, showered and dressed in clean clothes, Zoya takes the long way down to dinner. She swings by the staff wing, hoping to catch Leon in.

His door is slightly open, and she sees him inside, checking out his hairline in the mirror. She knocks lightly on the door.

'Come in!' he calls, patting his hair back into place and turning away.

The room is about the size of their room, but he has it all to himself. A small armchair and table have been crammed in near the window and a few small pots of struggling cacti adorn the windowsill.

He switches off the tinny radio. The mood seems awkwardly expectant now that the music has stopped.

Leon's clothes are draped here and there, dashing the room with colour. He busies himself folding things away into the drawer. She closes the door behind her, letting it shut with a loud click.

She hovers by the doorway waiting for him to look up.

'Oh, hey, listen, there's something I wanted to… mention.'

'Yes?'

He closes the drawer and leans, arms crossed, against the wall.

He has the same painted breeze block walls as everyone else but where the students might have stuck up posters, Leon's walls are studded with proper framed pictures: programmes, signed photographs of his dance heroes, souvenirs from his own career.

'Erm… I don't know what it means, but I saw something… odd in Toby's office the other day. I just wondered…'

'What did you see?'

'This will sound mad, but some kind of spy kit…?'

'And you just wondered if he's a spy…?'

Leon's eyebrow is raised quizzically, but he still manages to look annoyed.

'What would he be spying *on,* Zoya? This is a dance school.'

'Well, erm… us?'

'You think he's listening to your secrets?'

'No, not listening… but *looking* maybe…'

'He's not a pervert, Zoya; he's just got bad taste.'

Zoya narrows her eyes and cocks her head, not following his meaning.

'You know – the clothes, the glasses... Anyway, don't be so narrow-minded about people; I've known Toby for *years*. He's the best human you will ever meet.'

Leon manoeuvres past her toward the door as her cheeks start to flush. She is regretting bringing it up. Maybe Leon and Toby are the best of friends, maybe lovers. In any case, she is feeling acutely aware that she and Leon have actually only been friends for two minutes – if they even *are* friends; because surely being friendly with the students he mentors is just part of his job.

Now he is in the hall, gesturing with a curt hand curl for her to leave so he can lock up. She shuffles out of his room.

'You should be careful what you say about people, Zoya.'

'I'm sorry, I just... what was the thing I saw, then, do you think?'

'Is something wrong? I mean, what was your problem with Olivia yesterday?'

'I'm sorry?'

'I just didn't have you down as the selfish type, I suppose,' he is saying, walking off down the hall. 'Shows how wrong you can be about people,' he adds, muttering to himself.

Zoya stands where she is, her cheeks starting to burn now. She swallows.

'I was in class...'

Leon stops walking and pivots around to look back at her.

'Would it have killed you to miss it and take Olivia to see her sick sister? Anyway, doesn't matter.'

She stands, open-mouthed, starting to shake her head.

'I take it the tuition is off then?' she asks sharply.

He puts his hands to his hips and sighs, looking at his feet.

'I have things to do, Zoya. Anyway, Mya is your one-to-one tutor…'

He starts to walk off. She still can't believe it.

'*Selfish*?!' she exclaims.

He rounds the corner toward the main part of the building.

'Okay, I'm selfish then!' she shouts after his disappearing figure.

She stands there, angry, nowhere to go. The corridor is dimming with the sunset. She would have liked to be the one to storm off.

FEBRUARY

On a bright winter's day, Reed is ambling past a Victorian arcade back to his parked van.

The elegant stretch of shops features twisted posts and a glazed canopy and seems cheapened by the modern retailers installed inside. The newsagents he is leaving is brash with deals and convenience food and the ugly end of refrigerators.

Only the specialist cheese shop still maintains an air of sophistication, as does the gentleman shopper shuffling along the pavement following his decade-worn routine. Reed weaves around the cloud of cigar smoke that trails along in his wake.

'Reed! Hey, Reed!'

He doesn't recognise the voice but wheels around.

'*Reed!* Hi!'

She places herself right in front of him. It's Karen Harcourt, an old friend of Dan's who Reed met up in Edinburgh, nearly two years ago. She seems to have come from the direction of a car, parked, like his van, in a bay in front of the row.

'Karen!'

Reed is pleased to see her and hear someone use his name.

'So, what are you…?' he begins.

'Oh, my dad lives round here. I'm just moving some things from his attic to my new house, clearing some stuff out...' She gestures to a car that looks pretty well-laden with *stuff*. 'You know what, doesn't matter. It's good to see you, man! How are things? How's Dan? How's Zoya?'

'They're... good. So, are things all they cracked up to be on the force?'

'Yeah, it's... what I wanted. Challenging but rewarding, you know. Oh, hey, I have something for you!'

She steers him around the other vehicles and to her car. He waits while she unlocks it and rummages around in a pile on the back seat. Pigeons circle his feet as he waits.

'Here,' she says, thrusting a folded magazine into his hand.

He looks at it blankly.

'Recognise anyone?' she prompts, unfolding it to point out an article.

'Ian Rankin?'

Karen laughs.

'I knew you'd say that. But look – it's me and Zoya on a night out.'

Reed flips the magazine page straight and looks at the other photograph. There they are – in a colourful candid snap taken in a club used to illustrate an article about Edinburgh nightlife. They are dancing enthusiastically, sweat and happiness illuminating their faces, sharing a night out on the tiles and a good time.

Sometimes Reed almost wishes that Zoya had the kind of beauty that only *he* would secretly notice – and only because they are on the same wavelength – but there she is, all glowing and vibrant and attractive and on the pages of a magazine. He feels a drop in his stomach, the way he felt when he saw her dance audition – mesmerising and electric – all for those other people and not for *him*.

Karen is still talking.

'I was going to post it to her, but hey,' – she gestures at his presence as if she has waved a magic wand and made him appear – 'just the man!'

He smiles politely. Karen is opening her car door.

'I wish we had time to get a drink and a catch up together. I'd love to hear how everyone is, but' – she checks her watch – 'I've honestly got to be somewhere.'

Reed knows it must be true – Karen is nothing if not straight-talking.

'So, you'll pass it on to her for me?' she checks.

Reed is quiet for a moment. Karen won't know that they aren't a couple anymore.

'Oh, we're… she's… she's at a dance school…'

'Oh,' Karen gets into her car and flutters the fingers of her hand, 'just, you know, the next time you see her, I wanted her to have it, I…'

Suddenly Karen's eyes well up with glassy tears. Reed rests a hand on the car roof and leans toward her.

'Are you okay?'

'Yes.' She smiles and takes a deep breath and blinks the swell of emotion away. 'You know, it really meant something to me, those nights out after Fintan died. It might seem… inappropriate… but it did me the world of good.'

Reed nods.

'She's just one of those people, isn't she?' Karen continues. 'Leaves an impact. Pass it here a minute,' she adds, flicking the top off a biro. 'I'll write her a message.'

He lets her have the magazine back and watches while she scribbles something across the page.

This time, she passes it back to him wordlessly.

'I'll makes sure she gets it,' Reed says, moving back to let her close the door.

He watches from the pavement as Karen's red Polo begins to move. When she looks at him again, he pulls a confirmatory smile and salutes the folded magazine to his temple. Then, he watches Karen – and her stuff – drive away.

When she has gone, he unfolds the page to look at the message and stares at it for much longer than it takes to read the words. And, when he's done with his thinking and feeling, it seems like the after-image of Zoya's photo has seared itself onto his brain.

***

Zoya moves in slow motion, carving slices of air with arcing arms. She pushes into the ground and effects a twisting turn that starts low and rises through her body, flowing upwards through her lengthening spine until she feels like she has left the ground.

Instead of dinner, Zoya grabbed a banana and a juice and headed back to the studio block to get back to working on her routine.

The studio door opens, and Mya looks in.

'Oh sorry, I didn't know you were in here – no music.'

'What time is it?' Zoya asks, still swaying and turning.

'It's almost seven,' Mya says. 'Listen, I've got a group here. Do you mind if we come in and start our stretches?'

'No, not at all,' Zoya says, turning in another circle, the move approaching something that keeps running through her mind.

The dancers come in and start their bending and stretching. It makes no odds to Zoya, who keeps rehearsing. Months of immersive, non-stop dancing have made everyone's self-consciousness disappear.

The group don't pay her much attention and, as Zoya closes her eyes and tries to feel a movement she has been imagining, their conversation falls away.

She changes direction, rising with her feet, her spine, her arms, and then she tips forward in the balance, slowly changing her position in a nuanced, ever-expansive illusion of gliding descent.

***

Outside in the corridor, Zoya stops to check the noticeboard for unbooked studio time. A voice snaps her attention back to the door.

'I loved what you were doing in there, by the way,' Mya says, standing elegantly in the doorway.

Zoya can hear the group inside counting into their routine: ... *five, six, seven, eight...*

'Oh, thanks, it's not finished yet, I'm just...'

'It's about freedom, right?' Mya asks, though it sounds like more of a statement.

Zoya feels stunned and almost has to shake the feeling away. She suddenly feels naked; pinned by Mya's insight like a butterfly to a board. She feels her mouth hanging open but hasn't thought what to say.

Waves of thoughts rush over one another, filling her head with worries but not helping with a response. It's true but it sounds ridiculous – stated out loud. Who is *she* to try and dance about 'freedom' – with all her privileges in life?

Zoya runs the admissions photographs of her classmates through her mind's eye, like a slide show. Some of them could only attend the project because they won grants and bursaries – but not her.

She feels embarrassed that someone has seen so clearly the unnamed, unformed thing that she was dancing – even though expressing something is meant to be the whole point. She feels embarrassed that someone has named it for her: *freedom*. She finds herself saying yes.

'That's what it's all about, Zoya,' Mya adds. 'Treading your own path. See you in contemporary.'

Mya walks back into the studio, leaving Zoya alone in the shining corridor and lonely in her thoughts.

***

Reed is standing by his van at the side of a B-road. He closes the engine hatch and straightens up, feeling like an idiot. He has never run out of petrol before.

As he picks up the empty petrol can and starts walking along the grassy verge, he feels the shame of a man who has failed his vehicle. And for Reed, the 1973 late bay camper van is not just a vehicle, it's his home. This adds a level of guilt he is hoping that the long walk to a garage will evaporate rather than cement.

A car drives by, blaring its horn, and he catches sight of teenage lads jeering at him as they pass. He trudges on.

Time grinds along. Reed begins to feel like he's walking through treacle, not getting any nearer to his destination.

The traffic keeps up. The constant buzz of engines is annoyingly arrhythmic, and everything smells of exhaust. Grey plastic posts repeat the same pedantic traffic signs, making the long, boring walk feel infinite. The grass verge grows orange in the swelling light of the streetlamps blinking on. His paces tear at the grass, blade after blade catching at his dragging feet.

A sleek Ford Capri pulls up slightly ahead of him, gently gliding into the kerb. Reed keeps pacing forward, glancing subtly at the open window as he draws level with the car.

'That your camper van back there?' a voice says.

Reed peers into the car. He sees a man with brown, wavy hair leaning toward him from the driver's seat, and nobody else in the car.

'Yep,' Reed replies, blustering some confidence but secretly worried that the driver may have news about his van that he won't want to hear.

'Beautiful. You've kept her looking good,' the man says appreciatively.

Reed has never gendered his van but likes the compliment anyway.

'As is your Capri. Just taking my petrol can for a walk...' Reed says, attempting a joke.

He gestures awkwardly with the cannister, confessing his failure, and the man laughs kindly in response.

'I haven't imagined that there's a garage this way, have I?' Reed asks.

'Oh, hey man, get in. I'll give you a lift.'

'You sure?'

'No problem at all.'

***

Zoya emerges from the bathroom wearing her robe, rubbing her hair gently with a towel. Sharon is relaxing on her bed, flicking through a magazine.

Zoya smiles at her before padding around the room, sorting her stuff out, moisturising her face.

'I loved your routine today.'

Zoya stops and looks in the direction of the compliment. Sharon is watching her earnestly, her page-flicking fingers still.

'Thanks. How's yours coming along?'

'Good. It *feels* good, anyway.' Sharon raises herself up a bit on the bed. 'I'm looking forward to the show now.'

'Have you got people coming to see it?' Zoya asks.

Sharon closes the magazine and puts it down.

'I, er…, I hope so. I don't know.'

Zoya is torn between prying and not pushing it. Sharon hasn't been very forthcoming in the past. Zoya sits on the edge of her bed, tilts her head forward and works through her hair with the towel.

Sharon swings her own legs over the side of her mattress, mirroring Zoya's position.

'It's my… boyfriend - Alex,' she says.

'Oh? You never mentioned a boyfriend?' Zoya says, pausing the hair drying and looking up between damp curls.

Sharon plants her hands on the mattress, leaning forward, gripping the edge.

'Well, my ex… but… we've been talking recently. On the phone. I call him and we talk and I really think he's changed…' Sharon's wavering, babbling voice grows stronger and more fluid.

Zoya can tell that she's excited and is bubbling over with love and hope.

'So, I think I should invite him,' Sharon continues, 'I don't know…'

'Have you been meeting up with him?'

'No. He doesn't know where I am, actually. But… I really think I'd like him to come. I think if he saw me up there, dancing with the group… Do you know, when we met, he was watching me dance – in a club – he used to say my eyes shone when I was dancing. I just think, maybe he's changed. And maybe if he saw me up there… sees *me*…'

Sharon's sentence drifts away. She seems lost in her thoughts.

'I know what you mean.'

***

At the garage, Reed gets his petrol and feels relieved. He carries it across the forecourt and sets it down on some grass by the fence. He wonders if the Capri driver would be kind enough to give him a lift all the way back to his van – he seemed a helpful sort of chap.

The forecourt is acid-washed with floodlamps and the glare of the strip-lit shop; a strange, bright bubble between the fields and the road. The sky is still glowing with the sunset but looks dark in contrast.

He scans the forecourt, then spots the Capri driver by the pumps, checking his air.

The crawl of tyres at the entrance and exit is almost constant and the tarmac pulses with the thudding of opening and closing car doors. Reed tries not to look like he is obviously waiting around for a lift.

He watches a scruffy-looking dog hop through the back fence behind the garage. He's always had a thing about dogs. There's many a time Reed has thought about sharing his life on the road with a canine companion, but the thought is as far as he's got.

He watches the happy stray as it sniffs about the forecourt. Then he sees it focus shiny-eyed attention on the man squatting by his wheels. The dog pads closer, intrigued.

Reed watches, amused, as the stray surprises the man with his warm, doggy breath. The man shoos it away then crouches again by the car. The dog bounces away but then creeps – playfully - back. He presses his belly to the floor and starts wagging his tail, waiting for a repeat of the game.

Reed thinks this could be his cue to sidle over, stroke the dog's fluffy head and casually secure a lift back to his van. Before he can approach, the man aims a strong kick at the dog, booting it hard in the side.

Reed freezes. He hears the dog's yelp from where he stands. His instinct is to rush over and scoop up the poor animal, but it is already scrambling away through the undergrowth and losing itself in the dark fields.

Before the driver sees him, Reed picks up the heavy petrol can and strides away. He crosses to the other side of the road and marches angrily back in the direction of his van.

CHAPTER 15

One morning, Zoya manages to find her way onto the roof above the main hall and feels instantly at home.

From her vantage point, she can see the whole site – the buildings by the western fence, the decrepit outdoor stage, the thick wood beyond the residential block. She can see the hills in the distance and locates the dip where Rithling must lie.

The air is fresh and scentless, the landscape echo-laden and bare. The hard furrows of ploughed earth are seamed with frosted ridges like icing sugar. Copses of leafless trees resemble twisted tangles like spider nests. She can see the swell of pale, plaited fields stretching as far as the hills. The summits are emerging from a dusting of wispy clouds as the sunlight grows. She can hear the rolling chug of some small vehicle trundling along in a lane beyond the woods that she never knew was there.

In the grounds of the school, the swollen, slumping grasses weigh heavy with decay and dew; sharp curving patterns that remind her of the waves in Japanese art. Fancifully, she imagines that the main hall is an island, trapped by a sea of frozen ripples.

The night has barely frosted, and the rooftop is already dry. Tiny, sparkling crystals warmed by the trail of her footsteps are disappearing in the spreading sun.

Up on the rooftop, her arms resting on the wall, she can't help thinking of Dan and Reed and Edinburgh – and Marcus, freeing himself from misery – and a secret love resurfacing to the sun. She realises that she has become trapped in inside spaces again: the studios, the bedroom, the canteen.

She sees a cyclist coasting up the driveway: Luke Boyd returning from his early-morning ride. She puts herself in his position, imagining how good he must feel striking out alone like that, inhaling miles and miles of country air.

She watches his bike glide in a practiced arc through the car park and sees him dismounting on the move. He reminds her of Reed in some ways – none that Reed would recognise. Perhaps it's just the affinity with the open road.

Time to get to work, she thinks. Time to practice her routine.

When she runs through the choreography this time, she is thinking of vans and bikes and running footsteps, shooting, untethered, through the land. She thinks of Reed, unfettered by boundaries, opening door after door in his dreams. She thinks of Luke escaping each morning, beyond the narrow lanes. She thinks of the circling birds in the lofty distances above the hills. She channels the fleeting, infinite feeling she can only ever grasp for a moment – when she is drifting between flight and fall.

That feeling is the reason she throws herself from high places night after night after night... She wants to make that feeling last; to carry it from dream to day. She dares herself to fall higher and longer but it is always gone when she wakes.

She is channelling all this in her dancing now as she moves through her motif of floating descent.

The door from the stairwell bangs open and Leon Foster steps out.

'So, this is where you've been hiding?' he says, not stepping very far out onto the roof.

'I'm not hiding.'

He looks around at the wide view.

'No,' he agrees.

They both start talking at once.

'Did you want something?' she asks.

'Listen, I...' he begins.

They pause, looking at one another, until Leon steps closer.

'I wanted to apologise... For what I said last year. The truth is I...' he says.

'It's fine, I shouldn't...'

'No,' he says, firmly, stopping her sentence, 'I've missed you.'

He offers a tentative smile.

Zoya looks at him.

'I used to hero-worship you, you know, a little bit,' she confesses, a touch embarrassed, a touch amused by her former self.

'My "being worshipped" days are long gone...' he defers, with a self-deprecating little laugh. 'Forgive me?'

They look at one another, the friendship instantly back on.

'So, how's the routine?' he asks, landing on common ground. 'Are you all ready for the show?'

'Just going over a few things…'

'Show me?' he suggests, shuffling nearer again.

Zoya begins to dance for him.

'That's really wonderful, Zoya,' he says when she finishes. 'Can I make a suggestion?'

The way he says it isn't critical and she is, as ever, keen to absorb any dance wisdom that he can send her way.

'What?' she asks, eagerly.

'You know this bit?' He shows her. 'Have you thought about changing it for something like this?'

And then he shows her an alternative. It changes the move – but changes it into something good.

Zoya feels the way she felt in that Bramchester school hall that day; an electrified tingle shooting around her body from the touch of his hand.

'You're a genius. Thanks,' she says, accepting the new choreography, lit up by his attention, happy to have her friend back in her life.

***

Val Staines is in her living room, applying shiny purple lipstick to her uneven pout. A *Sounds of the Sixties* radio programme is playing quietly in the kitchen.

The room features a marble-effect fireplace, soft carpet and cream leather sofa packed with regimented cushions. Everything in the house is shiny smooth or seriously plush and smells of cleaning products and Benson & Hedges. The oversized clock flashes gold on the mantelpiece, the swinging rotary pendulum twinned in the mirror behind.

She closes the lipstick and checks her reflection. She might try out a new hair colour, she thinks, feathering her fringe. She checks her roots at the temple and resolves to make an appointment for, well, anytime. She smiles to herself thinking about it – *free as a bird.*

There's a knock at the door. When she opens it, a rangy man is standing on the doorstep, his arm raised to lean on the lintel.

'Hello, Auntie Val,' he says.

She folds her arms.

'Alex fucking Belasis!' she exclaims by way of icy greeting, 'I'm not your aunt.'

'Come on, he must be expecting me. Where is the cunt?' he says, pressing his body into the doorway.

Val furrows her brow, searching his face, then warms to the realisation that she has him at a disadvantage.

'Don't you know?' she asks.

Alex pushes past her and into the front room. She finds him standing, tall and agitated, on the cream carpet, restless eyes dashing all around.

'Are you about to tell me he isn't here?' he chides, already tired of their short conversation.

Val watches as he paces about erratically, looking for something, peering into the back garden, checking on his Capri parked out the front.

'Mick isn't anywhere,' she tells him, when he looks at her. 'Died of a heart attack six months ago. *Thank fuck.*'

Alex takes in the information, an accusation frozen on his lip.

'Explains why you haven't seen him up north recently doesn't it?' She snorts. 'Didn't anyone tell you? Ah,' she adds, sarcastically.

He watches as she rummages in a drawer, then strolls back toward him and presses a printed order of funeral service into his chest with a small shove.

He looks at the evidence, thinking quickly.

'So, where's my money?'

'What money? Alex, you must be smoking the wrong weed. You're paranoid. After everything Mick did for *you…*'

'Don't give me that,' Alex snaps, exasperated.

He knows she's never been the innocent little lady – not like Sharon who he always kept out of things.

'Well, I've ruled out everyone else,' he says, the tone of aggression giving way to uncertainty. He defaults to expecting her motherly advice.

Val revels in his predicament.

'Listen, I don't know who took your money, but Mick's been dead since August. Seems a pretty tight alibi to me.'

She puts one hand on Alex's arm and the other around his back and starts guiding him back into the hall.

'You seem confused. Best thing that ever happened to me – Mick dying. Means I don't need to put up with pricks like you anymore.' She opens the door to the street. 'Get out.'

He finds himself stepping back out of the house.

'Nobody else knew,' he says, thinking aloud.

He sees a softly mocking look in Val's eyes now.

'Really? *Nobody?*' she says, waiting for him to fuck off.

Alex's face falls, the penny slowly dropping: *Sharon.* He never even considered her until now.

He balls his fist in anger. Then he punches Val hard in the face.

In the hallway, Val clutches at the door to steady herself. He hasn't knocked her over, but she really, *really* needs to sit down. She can hear his footsteps storming away to his car.

On the floor of the hallway, she holds trembling hands to her face. There is blood at her nose now and she shuts her eyes tight to deal with the pain.

She hears him start the engine and squeezes open her good eye to watch the orange Capri driving away. She stays down, holding a hand protectively over the side of her face. And then she starts to laugh – a gravelly chuckle. That was the last of the idiot men to come calling.

If this is all she has to put up with in return for no more Mick and no more Mick's 'friends', she thinks, then it's a small price to pay.

She decides on auburn lowlights at the hairdresser next time – when her face is presentable again.

Behind her palm, the black eye begins to shine.

CHAPTER 16

On the day of the show, the dancers are being shuttled to Kedbury Theatre in rehearsal order. Toby and Luke are doing the driving in shifts. It's almost like they have organised this before, which they have, Zoya thinks – every year, the same.

She sits at the back of the minibus looking out of the window and mentally running through her steps. *If you don't know your routine by now…* people keep saying – but it's a phrase that cuts both ways; depends which side of the river you are coming from.

Zoya looks around the bus and sees nervous excitement bubbling under all the casual conversations. She sits quietly at the back. Sharon, Sandy, Tilda and Lauren are already at the theatre.

The coach slips through Rithling, pressing on in a new direction. When they pass the small Savertown supermarket on the outskirts, everywhere becomes somewhere that Zoya has never been. The performance isn't for hours and hours yet, but as the market town she has come to know evaporates behind them, she can feel the churn of growing nerves.

Apparently, the annual Valentine Show is well attended by a supportive and forgiving local audience – *they keep telling them* – and everything – *they keep saying* – is going to go well.

Hills rise around them. Zoya watches the high crest looming on the other side of the narrow river, the stark sunlight revealing rocky folds and winter birds.

The minibus crosses a thick, iron bridge and Zoya sees a bright flash of rushing river below. She is thrilled and surprised by the depth of the drop. For the rest of the journey, her mind is buzzing with plans that have nothing to do with remembering her steps.

***

Zoya navigates her way through the wings, avoiding the rasping unfinished edges and the darkest corners filled with dust. She edges around grubby cables and ropes to a spot at the side of the stage, where she quietly steps from side to side, stretching her calves and keeping herself warmed up.

She can hear the dancers' feet on the creaking boards and the music being played through the speakers, but no sound from the audience; no clues that anyone is out there at all. She stays hidden behind the flat and watches the dancers perform their routine.

She can see Clare, Jo and Gemma on stage, moving in the spotlights. Beyond them, only a dark hush. She's been told that the little regional theatre is full, but the invisible audience must be paying quiet, rapt attention, or else they have all gone home.

She watches her friends perform their routine, willing them through the tricky parts. Sharon isn't with them, though. She was there for the dress rehearsal but Zoya hasn't seen her to talk to since. She wonders what happened. The three remaining dancers have reshuffled themselves into new positions, closing the gap.

Zoya's attention drifts away again, mentally running through her routine for the thousandth time, carefully rehearsing the new move that Leon bestowed on her up on the roof. She comes to, recognising that the previous piece is ending: three female bodies gracefully coming to rest on the boards. The music ebbs away in an inhale-exhale of pauses and is over.

The applause begins before the dancers get up to take their bows; a sudden reminder of all the people sitting out there in the dark.

Zoya's heart races. She is meant to jog on from the wings just as the previous group dash away at the other side. She takes a breath. This is good, she reminds herself: she loves to dance, she was lucky to get into the programme, she is confident in her routine.

She finds her position on the stage, feeling, at once, very alone and very watched. She feels the stage lighting change and listens for her music to begin.

***

The spotlight fades away slowly as Zoya moves through her motif for three... and two... and one last time. The lighting has been designed to make her movement seem infinite to the audience and, judging from the long seconds she spends waiting in the darkness, it probably does. It feels like there's really nobody there at all. The applause begins – faltering, swelling – and the lights come up. She dips her head in a modest bow and jogs lightly off the stage.

***

One person in the audience remains motionless: Reed, awestruck and crestfallen in the dark. He is so caught up in admiration that he has entirely forgotten to clap.

He wants to tell everyone that he knows her, that *he* has danced with her and *more*, that she is *his* – but she isn't – and it has never been more clear. He wants her dance to carry on and for all the people to disappear. He wants to run backstage and find her, but just sits still in his chair. He had planned to surprise her after the show, but now knows – *knows* without deciding – that he will just slope away into the night and she will never know that he was here.

***

Backstage and exhilarated, Zoya's body processes the adrenaline. She paces around and into a changing area, kicking the warmth down through her legs and feet. She finds herself alone now and remembers her breathing and stretches.

It seemed to go well. She has no memory of messing any of it up – but no memory of it happening *at all*. She collects her bag from the numbered hooks and starts pulling on her jogging bottoms.

Zoya's pulse has lengthened but there's still something catching at her breath. She examines her physiology – no, nothing seems amiss. She doesn't feel right though – feels like there is something heavy in the pit of her stomach. She puts on her sweater, now noticing the fire escape chill. She lets her hair down, ruffling her curls and rubbing her fingers across her scalp. It feels as though the adrenaline high is leaving her body, draining away to reveal a strange, dark vacuum in the depths of her as the excitement subsides.

'That was great, Zoya. Well done.'

She looks to the doorway and the voice. Mya is standing there, smiling.

'Thanks. Was it okay?'

'Didn't you hear the audience?'

'I…'

'Why did you change that section toward the end, though? I think I preferred it the first way. Doesn't matter – the audience loved it. Well done!'

Mya bustles away to marshal the next group of nervous dancers into the correct running order, leaving Zoya on her own with a leaden, sinking feeling that won't go away.

***

I leave the dance school through the main hall and out through the double doors. The night flows around me thickly; grey mists diffusing the moonlight, touching my skin like invisible velvet.

As I spy Luke's bike against the wall, I think for a second of taking it; the appeal of a long, easy cycle ride through the dream-warm night draws my imagination along the shadowy lanes of trees and hilly vistas of my own private country. But I leave it where it is. If I borrowed Luke's bike, I would have to leave it somewhere else and then he wouldn't have it when he needed it for his morning ride.

I double my pace and meet the lane at a jog, heading for the town. I lengthen my stride, enjoying the power and freedom of my own two legs. I emerge from the tree tunnel, my easy dream-energy and my dance fitness and the gradual slope of the road making me feel like I am flying down the hill. The moon brightens. By the time the streetlamps appear, languidly placed along an emerging pavement, I slow to walk and look around.

I pass the Red Dragon Chinese restaurant, turn at the camping shop at the corner and enter the town square. I make my way up to the path and stop where it bridges the steps. I know that, far below the town's edge, there is a winding, deep-cut river moving through the valley and the night.

I look over the edge. The riverside steps that lead down to the low road by the water descend below me and I pause to consider the drop. I keep walking. I need somewhere that is wide open and endless and free.

I can make out the high hilltops emerging from the gloaming in silvery moonlight. If only I could transport myself right up there without a climb. I look around the valley and across the star-freckled sky.

This is the high path that skirts the edge of town and I know where it joins the main road – just before the iron bridge.

I remember crossing the ravine earlier, on the way to the theatre, and being shocked by the depth of it; the view falling away to shadows, even in the day. I walk on and on.

I keep moving in the direction of the bridge, following the high path through the valley. Soon, I start to see it in the distance: the curved, iron span of the bridge that nobody thinks about – but me. It's still a distance away but growing clearer with every minute of my walk.

I see something in the middle distance – a figure rising from the bank. He unfolds his long legs slowly and steps out onto the path as if to show himself without startling me. I would know that silhouette anywhere.

He stands, waiting, as I approach, and I can't help but smile. We draw closer and I see that Reed is smiling too.

'Hi, Zoya,' he says.

I purse one side of my mouth a little, working things out.

'This isn't a coincidence, is it?'

He shuffles a foot and looks back up at me with that small, flickering grin.

'Nope. I came to see your show.'

'Oh.'

I don't know why this would make me feel… *something*, but it does.

'Did you enjoy it?' I ask.

In the shadowy dawn light, I watch his expression. He looks like he is remembering, actively thinking himself back to the moment so he can give me an honest response.

'I don't know,' he says, simply.

We both laugh.

'So, what's the plan? Where are you heading?' he asks, moving the topic onwards.

He must have caught my eyes darting toward the bridge, because then he turns to examine it. He looks back at me with an emphatic tilt of his head.

'You're not serious?'

I know he isn't telepathic, but he seems to know my plan. I open my mouth to answer, but I'm not sure what to say.

'You are *not* jumping off that bridge.'

His sentence lands halfway between incredulous and forbidding.

'That's your thing, isn't it? The jumping.'

I start walking again, then feel his hand lightly on my shoulder.

'Just over that rise, there's a creepy old house. Want to explore it with me? You should see it; looks like a haunted house from a movie…'

I keep walking, casually and slowly, and feel his hand slipping from my shoulder. I hear his feet shuffling over the scrabbly stone path, following me.

'I'm going this way,' I tell him.

'Oh.'

I hear his feet stop and, when I turn to look at him, he seems physically dejected. It's not even a jokey little pose he has put on to amuse me.

'You can come too,' I say, not stopping.

I look at the path curving toward the main road – still some way to go. He catches up with me.

'You looked amazing up there,' he says, his voice deep and quiet and earnest at my side.

'Thanks, I…'

'It must have felt good,' he says.

'Actually, it didn't feel as good as it should have,' I say, surprising myself.

'Not as exciting as all the night-time base jumping, I suppose?'

'It's just that… I had a different routine and I… shouldn't have changed it. Never mind. Anyway, nothing feels like falling and falling and never touching the ground.' I look up at him. 'It's flying.'

'Nope. Not for me, I'm afraid,' he answers, as if declining an invitation. 'I *like* touching the ground. Not as much of a thrill seeker as you are.'

'*Daredevil*, you said in Edinburgh… But that's not *it*.'

'No? What is it?'

I close my eyes, turning my face to the sky.

'Freedom,' I say. 'It's freedom.'

When I open my eyes again, the road bridge comes into focus, illuminated by the dawn light falling between the hills. I can see the colours of the painted ironwork against the monochrome shades of the dying night.

Reed's footsteps pause again.

'I have to say, that's one scary-looking bridge. I mean, how deep do you think the ravine is? Don't you think it's dangerous?'

I press on, closer and closer.

'How can it be dangerous?' I ask. 'If we fall, we wake!'

My voice rings out in the still air.

'But… what if we don't?' he says. 'I taught you that trick so you can wake up from the dreaming any time you want. It's only meant to be a short fall – so you get that sensation and your brain wakes up. It was never meant to be… plunging off rooftops and monuments and castles and… into ravines.'

I have reached the edge of the bridge and am touching the cool metal of the barrier, waiting for him.

'Well, it hasn't killed me yet,' I answer brightly. 'You know, I've been training my brain to accept it – I can fall higher and longer before it even wakes me up. And then I'm awake in my bed, perfectly safe and comfortable.'

I lean against the bridge casually, watching him approach.

'And you never have any… ill effects?'

'No.'

He leans a long arm on the metal siding next to me.

'I need it,' I say.

Reed turns himself to face the valley, looking over the bridge and the dark cut of the river and the view. He looks serious.

'But you've heard of mirror neurons,' he says. 'What we observe happening to other people – or happening to ourselves in a dream – has real physiological effects on us, on anyone, in real life.'

He walks off toward the centre of the bridge.

'Where are you going?' I ask, following.

He glances back, working up a comedic expression.

'To the *ravine of doom*…'

We reach the centre of the bridge.

'There's no way in the world I would jump off this bridge – in the dreaming or otherwise,' he says. 'You can't seriously be planning to?'

I shrug slightly, smiling back, but just as serious.

'Watch me.'

Then I start checking out the struts and testing the giant rivets for use as footholds. It doesn't seem so difficult to climb up onto the barrier top.

'Er, no, no, I don't think I could even do that,' he says, turning away, as if to make eye contact with another, more rational, witness who might talk me out of it, even though we are the only two people in the world.

'Come on, don't do it,' he says, appealing directly to me again. 'I mean, we have all *this*' – he looks around, encompassing everything in one sweeping, gestural glance – '*any* time we fall asleep. What more freedom could you possibly want?'

I feel a creeping chill inside of me.

'You'll never understand. Give me a leg up?'

'No,' he says firmly. 'No, I'm not doing that.' He has a frightened look on his face now. 'In fact, if you climb up there, I'm pulling you down.'

He puts his hands on his hips and I notice his shoulders spreading in the silhouette. He's slender, yes, but still a man; taller and bigger and stronger than I am. He *could* stop me if he wanted to, could pull me back or throw me off.

'It's not up to you,' I say.

He breaks his pose, moving his weight onto one leg and running a hand across his forehead.

'Please, Zoya, please.' He's gesturing toward me now, open-palmed and panicky. 'I mean, what's even at the bottom of that drop? Have you even looked?'

At that moment, an early ray of sunshine pokes its way through the thin clouds and falls across his face as if to emphasise his point.

Together, we notice the sunshine and the lightening rocks and stay silent. We look at the pleated heights of the valley bathed in new light. The slopes cup pools of lime-bright dawn and we see towering perches and century-scattered scree. Below us sounds the secret song of the river; mossy rocks bubbling as water laps its banks.

The ravine leads our gaze to the next glimpse of brightening valley and the next; the beautiful, majestic stillness of a landscape peopled by only two.

I lean my forearms on the barrier top. Reed joins me in the pose, though his feet, unlike mine, remain on the tarmac.

We keep looking along the valley, admiring the calm beauty of rising hills and etched crevices patterning the slopes. We follow the descent down toward the darkly swelling river and both freeze at the same time.

'What's that?' Reed says, in an unfamiliar, cracking voice.

At the bottom of the slope, on a rocky outcrop, almost beneath the bridge itself, is a dash of fabric.

It could be something washed up by the river, except, when I look at it, *really* look at it, I can see that it is above the waterline and has fallen from above.

I see a technicolour blue I recognise, stark against the grey rocks. I see the pattern flashing through my mind. Bright blue speckled white.

I hear my voice as if someone else is talking.

'*I* bought her that dress.'

Zoya and Reed are standing outside the police station, leaning against the mottled, bumpy wall. They are standing by a tangle of dead weeds and windswept rubbish that has accumulated on the paving near the gutter.

From where they stand, around the side of the station, only a narrow view across the river is revealed between buildings, making the slice of bland rocky cliff seem to loom menacingly over the small, insignificant town.

Reed leans his head back against the dimpled stone, sucking from a cigarette. He doesn't know what's worse – seeing an actual dead body on the ground in front of you, or imagining it, from the clothing and the blood. No, he *does* know which is worse.

He can hear the chugging and beeping of a reversing lorry delivering to the pub along the road, but the squabbling magpies in a nearby tree are louder and more irritating.

He exhales and rolls his head against the wall to look at Zoya. He has a sudden memory of a better time; a different wall in a different town and a thrilling first touch, scored by the sounds of the sea.

'Fuck!' Zoya exclaims, angrily.

Reed's eyes shoot open as her voice yanks him out of the memory.

'I still can't believe it,' she says.

He can feel her anger like an aura. He rubs his eyes. They have been awake since dawn, waking and reconvening at the police station, though only Zoya went inside.

By the time Zoya's police interview is over and they are taking a breather outside, the sun is shining more strongly and the town bustles in its normal, provincial way; oblivious. Reed and Zoya stand, winded, nowhere to go. Now, they are left feeling purposeless, just time and space stretching around them as the horrible news sinks in.

The sun shines too strongly into his eyes, so he squints them closed, taking another drag of the cigarette. He bends a knee and rests his foot against the wall. He exhales, the smoke co-mingling with a sigh.

'Can you believe those policemen?' Zoya spits, looking at him with flashing eyes. 'Did you hear what they were saying to each other when I came out?'

Reed watches her steadily.

'Of course they would assume she just threw herself off there!' she snaps sarcastically.

Reed pauses with the cigarette almost to his lips.

'Because we're all suicidally crazy, aren't we – *women*?'

He knows it is different, but Zoya had, just before they discovered Sharon's body, been planning to do just that – but he's not going to say that now.

'That was different,' she says, quickly, guessing at his thoughts nonetheless.

She leans closer and takes the cigarette from his fingers. He has rarely seen her smoke – never during waking life, anyway. She takes a drag and exhales to the blank heavens with an odd look on her face. It looks like she is chastising a god he knows she doesn't even believe in.

Reed drops his hand to his side and wiggles his fingers into his jeans pocket.

'Do you know… when I was in the interview room,' she says, 'and I was telling them about that ex-boyfriend she mentioned, they kept trying to say she might have provoked him – *provoked*!'

She hands him back the cigarette. They are apparently sharing now. Reed bites his lip.

'But it might have been him,' he says.

'Yes, yes it *might*,' Zoya agrees, 'but "provoked" sounds to me like they are already trying to blame her for her own murder.'

Reed has his smoke, pausing to feel the effects before answering.

'We don't know what happened yet.'

'No, we don't. But I know she was *happy* – she was happy and she was doing something she loved and she was looking forward to the dance show.'

She turns her face toward Reed and he holds the shrinking cigarette to her lips.

They stand there, thinking.

'Do you think they suspect *us*?' Reed wonders.

'We weren't even there.' Then Zoya lets out a loud, guttural cry. 'They don't give a fuck, you know. If a woman is killed. The papers do – they *love* it, sells papers. But the police don't. They just think it's normal. A normal part of life.'

'Frank doesn't,' Reed observes, and the reference to Shilly-on-Sea and old family friends gives Zoya a pang of something she didn't know she felt.

'No, *not all policemen*. But…' Zoya shakes her head a little. 'You don't understand.'

She pushes herself away from the wall and starts to walk off. Reed looks after her, about to follow.

'I'm beginning to,' he says.

***

The next morning, everyone is sitting quietly in the atrium canteen; a sullen picture of damp hair, red noses, wet eyes, slumped bodies, unshaven jaws and slept-in clothes. Some of the breakfast trays look barely touched; other people haven't even tried to eat. Some of the dance students are wrapped in thick jumpers or blankets as if soft textiles could protect them from the awful news.

Nobody will be dancing today.

Between the scraping of chairs and the clatter of cutlery fall slow, sniff-filled silences. Even the balling of tissues can be heard.

It's hard to look at people. Zoya examines the pendant lampshades – high orbs out of reach and thick with dust. Sobs and sighs rebound around the room, clashing in echo with the concrete columns that reach up to the ceiling. Someone's foot starts tapping weakly, against the floor.

She shifts position and pushes away the overripe banana still in front of her. The smell is cloying and makes her feel sick.

'So, what we have to decide in the next few days, collectively,' Meredith says gently, 'is how to proceed with the programme. It might be that we decide on a break and shorten the final semester – or it might be that the best thing would be just to carry on.'

Jerrod is with her.

'If any of you choose *not* to continue, that will be fine, but we would urge you not to make your decision right away – while everything is raw,' he adds.

Today they are both sitting on the bottom step. It doesn't matter that not everyone can see them, because many of the students are just staring at the ground or off into space. Zoya finds herself studying the metal bannisters that range along the staircase.

She feels a warm hand lightly placed on her forearm. She looks to see Leon, who has been sitting there all along. Nobody says anything.

'We *have* to carry on.'

Zoya is surprised to hear her own voice calling out strongly in the silence.

'We don't *have* to,' Leon says, beside her, taking his hand off her arm and shifting in his seat.

She looks at him, and then at everyone.

'We do! For Sharon's memory. She put *herself* into some of that choreography. She deserves to have that...

presence… in the end-of-year show. Not that doing the show matters, really – except now it really does.'

Zoya looks around from face to face, most of which stay downturned and glum. She sees Clare tear up and glance away. Jerrod is standing now.

Zoya sits up straighter. 'I'm just saying that… I think we should honour Sharon by carrying on in her memory. She loved what we were doing…'

Meredith rises regally.

'I agree.'

'Okay,' Jerrod says, taking control, 'here's what we'll do. We'll vote and, if we have enough people, we'll carry on with the programme as it is. When shall we have the vote?'

'Now,' Sandy says, and everyone seems to agree.

'Perhaps we should vote anonymously,' Meredith suggests, but nobody seems to want to.

If anyone says the T.E.A.M. thing, Zoya thinks, she will throw something through the plate glass.

'Right,' Jerrod says. 'Everyone okay with us having the vote now? You don't have to say what your reasons, thoughts or feelings are, and nobody is going to judge anyone for them – we're only interested in numbers. And if the majority vote to carry on, it doesn't mean that individuals can't have a bit of time off; whatever you need, we'll work something out.'

People manage to muster some assenting noises and nods.

'Okay,' he says, 'raise your – no, stand up, if you vote to proceed with the programme as planned.'

There is a rumble of chair legs and footsteps as basically everyone stands. Not absolutely everyone, though, Zoya notices. Leon remains seated by her side. She looks down at him and catches a strange expression on his face, just before he turns away.

She doesn't mean to be judgemental, but his choice seems odd. She happens to know that he was out there, performing on a West End stage, the very night after his father died, whereas the Midsummer Show is still months away, and is just this provincial thing, just a nothingy little project, just them.

'Oh, right,' she says softly, remembering something he told her. 'You're going to audition for that job, then?'

He looks back at her, glaring, and slowly begins to stand. Maybe she was wrong.

But he keeps on walking – away from the table and across the long expanse of parquet floor.

'Right – leaving just when we need you?!' she calls after him, surprised again by the loudness of her voice.

Leon doesn't look around. Then she feels it – the ice-cold mood of the room as everyone judges her for judging. She looks from face to face.

Then she is struck by the crystal-clear memory of those three women's bodies landing on the stage and the missing dancer and she can see it in her imagination – Sharon's slow-motion fall from the bridge to the deathly rocks below.

Leon keeps on walking: a relaxed, casual stroll that infuriates her even more. He reaches the door to the corridor. She takes a breath to shout after him again.

'It's just abstract for men, isn't it? You don't *have* to care!'

The swinging door bangs closed behind him and he keeps going and is gone.

Zoya turns around to face everyone but can sense before she sees it – a room full of people standing behind her but not a single person on her side.

***

A few days later, Reed and Zoya are standing outside the main building by his van.

A couple of students walk by and look at them. Nobody is introduced.

'Are you sure you don't want to come with me?' he asks, after they pass. 'I can take you anywhere you want. Or nowhere in particular.'

When he says the last bit, he is specifically thinking of the rambling road trip they took, just the two of them in the camper van, when they were together – but she doesn't seem to follow his train of thought.

'No.' She declines his offer, gently. 'I'm staying here and carrying on.'

He looks at her with narrowing eyes as if to see through her outer shell, give her another chance to get out.

'You sure?'

'Yeah.'

They find themselves looking at the glassy facade of the main hall. Shadowy figures are moving around inside.

'You *sure* you're sure?' he quips, in a rising cadence.

Zoya looks at her feet.

'Yes.'

Then she looks up and away to the hidden valley and the hills.

'For Sharon,' she adds.

'Do we know more about what happened yet?' Reed asks.

Zoya's expression twitches.

'No, but I'm going to find out.'

Reed realises that, for Zoya, staying on at the New Movement School has taken on a whole new dimension.

She looks back at him.

'You get off now,' she says.

He tries one last time.

'*Sure* you don't want to leave with me?'

She makes a firm, close-mouthed smile.

'Sure.'

He nods once to show his acceptance, and then, before any sort of goodbye kiss or hug can happen or *not happen*, he finds his feet taking him toward the van.

'Okay, stay safe!' he calls as he is climbing inside.

He says it like a jokey sign-off but they both know he means it too.

Zoya smiles weakly and touches her first and second finger to her forehead like a salute.

'See you soon,' he says, finally, and shuts the door.

Zoya watches the van as it disappears along the drive. Inside the cabin, Reed makes a random decision to take a left turn at the junction and disappears into the lane.

MARCH

From her table in the café Zoya can see them leaving. She watches the minibus pull out of the car park and trundle through the square without her. None of them seems to notice her sitting quietly at the booth table, watching through the glass.

First, she had declined to go shopping with Gemma and Lauren, opting instead to meander around the market town, lost in her thoughts, thinking mostly of Sharon.

Then, she had told Toby that she would be staying on and making her own way back later, as he leant by the bus, ready to drive everyone back. She sees him now, at the wheel as the vehicle passes by. He seems as placid as ever, as if nothing has happened, as if nobody had died.

She watches the minibus disappear without her.

Her gaze drifts up to the colourless sky, before eventually registering a grey gull wheeling and gliding below the clouds. A lone gull, she thinks – so far from the sea.

She thinks about Toby driving that night, imagining the same minibus and the same Toby at the wheel – like an after-image – reconstructing the day of Sharon's death in her mind. He is still the last known person to have seen her, dropping her off here in Rithling, in the four-hour gap between the rehearsal and the show, the sole passenger with her personal errand to run.

He can't have been the actual last person to have seen her alive, but nobody else has come forward yet. For the moment, Sharon's timeline sticks at the town square drop-off, disappearing to nothing and to death.

Zoya feels for Toby; having had to record an alibi, having had to be interviewed by the police about the death of a friend. He had, of course, been taking the opportunity to go and see his mum. She thinks of the gentle innocence of the hazy net curtains, the soft leather of the trunk of memories, the lullaby whistle of the kettle on the hob.

Of course, the fact that Marianne couldn't remember or confirm it doesn't make anyone doubt him. There are medical records to support the fallibility of her memory nowadays. It's just... unfortunate.

It's unfortunate, too, that his timeline is also left hanging, tangling up with Sharon's like that, part of the line of her last movements that leads to the bridge and the jagged, blood-stained rocks.

It can't feel good to be knotted up in it like that, she thinks. Or maybe the shock and the grief are enough to push everything else out.

The gull floats left and right, up and away from her, a small speck evaporating into the high mists.

A plate is placed on the table in front of her. She sees a scone that's far too big to eat. She looks at it – all puffy and crumbly and soft. She has no appetite to eat it but that's not why she ordered it anyway. She can see Sharon now, in her mind's eye, cutting one in half for them to share.

'Your friend not with you?'

The chirpy voice cuts into her thoughts. Zoya looks up to see a waiter she recognises, and his smiling, friendly eyes.

'Oh...' Zoya swallows. 'Er, no...'

To do something else with her mouth – something other than talk about Sharon's death again – Zoya picks up her coffee cup for a sip, the drink already growing cold.

'Terrible about that woman, isn't it?' the man goes on, half perching on the wooden arm of the other bench.

Zoya looks at him slowly, raising her eyes warily to take in his expression. He really doesn't seem to know.

'You must have heard about it,' he says. 'It's awful, that poor woman who threw herself off the bridge...'

His eyes are flitting left and right as he watches people passing in the square outside, perhaps contemplating which of them might be capable of doing the same. He stops his people-watching, becoming aware of Zoya's steady gaze.

'What is it?'

'That was *her* – Sharon Surtees,' Zoya says quietly.

His eyes widen and he stands.

'It was Sharon's body in that ravine.'

He starts to shake his head, a tiny movement.

'But... the police came around with a photograph... it wasn't... your friend.'

'No, it *was*,' Zoya says, firmly.

He looks confused.

Then Zoya scrabbles around in her bag for her own photograph; the one Tilda had taken of Sharon and her in the canteen; the one in the packet she has just picked up that she had put off getting developed and having to look at. She finds it in the set of prints and hands it over quickly, managing to *not* look at it too much, managing to *not* look at Sharon's happy, living face.

He holds the photograph lightly, but with both hands, staring at it.

'Are you sure? No, of course you're sure, but... she didn't look like this in the police photograph – *that* woman looked skinny, the mouth was different... I would have recognised her if they had shown me this.'

'No,' Zoya says, calmly. 'It's the same woman. I know the police got their photo from the dance school's record – from registration. It's... it was her.'

He looks ashen now. He hands back the photograph gently.

'Oh, my god. I'm so sorry. I remember you two coming in here. I'm so sorry...'

Zoya takes the photograph and tucks it neatly away in the inside pocket of her bag, still not looking at it. She looks at him, nodding instead of formulating words.

'Thanks,' she says eventually.

'I'm so sorry I brought it up like that... I hadn't recognise her...'

Zoya nods again and he retreats from the table.

'Oh, Brian,' Zoya says, calling him by the name she has read on his name tag before but never had reason to say out loud.

He pauses and looks back at her.

'But you would have recognised her if they had shown you *this* photograph?' Zoya asks.

'Yes,' he says.

When Zoya looks out of the window, she can hear him walking away.

Then she looks up to the shaded sky. She puts her hand back in her bag and touches the edge of the photograph, just to know it is there.

At least now she knows that there is something she can do. It's just, right now, she can't help feeling afraid of it; that photograph – their happy, smiling faces, Sharon innocently laughing and not knowing the awful fate that lay ahead.

She decides to tackle the scone, resolving to eat just a little bit, just to defeat the pressure of it – sitting there in front of her, all significant and laden with memories. As she drags the plate across the tabletop, the napkin slips off the edge and into the narrow space between the glass window and the wooden platen that edges the booth. She retrieves it from the gap, pulling up a crumpled piece of paper that she recognises with it.

It is a ticket to the Valentine Show.

***

In a different county, Reed is having his own snack break, sitting on the edge of the open cabin door, his feet on the grassy verge. He bites into an apple and looks out on a pleasant view of fields. A soft breeze cools his face.

He finishes the apple and tosses the core into a patch of shrub. He folds up the newspaper that has been resting on his knees and turns back toward the cabin, aiming the paper at a pile on the side. When he throws, the whole pile slips to the floor.

He watches the small avalanche of papers and magazines as if it is happening in slow motion, then sighs and clambers back inside the van.

He sets about tidying the fallen pile, standing when one particular item finds its way into his hands. He dusts off the magazine he took from Karen for Zoya and feels guilty. He hadn't got around to passing it on. He should find somewhere safe to keep it until he can.

In the face of everything that happened, it seems like nothing – but isn't. Holding the magazine in his hands, he feels the emotional weight of it: an unfinished task; another small way of letting someone down.

He puts it in a drawer for safekeeping, and, as he places it carefully inside, his fingers touch Zoya's notebook, the one he has been carrying around for months and months. He picks it up and flicks through the pages, finding a blur of names and places. It turns out to be her address book, he realises. Odd that she never mentioned missing it at all.

Reed starts to suspect his subconscious of making a little shrine to their lost relationship and resolves to give it back.

He thinks of their goodbye at the dance school and how those other students had seemed cool with her. He thinks of Zoya trapped there with them, all isolated behind the trees.

It would probably give her a boost to see the magazine article and have her notebook back – full of friends' phone numbers and decorated with happy, family smiles.

He taps the spine of the address book against his brow, a wild, new idea taking flight. He sits on the bed and spreads out his *A–Z* – just checking something, just cross-referencing the address book and the map.

Then he pulls the door closed, slides into the driver's seat and manages a U-turn in the narrow country road.

CHAPTER 19

The next day, Zoya is in the charity shop watching as the assistant and manager study the photograph. She has slipped out of classes at the dance school to take it around Rithling and is running out of places to ask.

'I don't think so, no,' the manager says, returning Zoya's gaze.

'Are you sure?'

The volunteers are shaking their heads, their expressions sympathetic. The manager hands the photograph back to her.

'You didn't see her that day? She might have been with a man? Maybe out in the square? I mean, I'm not saying she came into the shop but…?'

Despite a day full of 'no, I'm sorry', there is still a heartbreaking hopefulness to her tone of voice.

Reluctantly, she takes the photograph back.

'No. I'm sorry.'

'Look, the police did ask us about her already,' the assistant adds. 'We've already said… I'm sorry.'

Zoya slips the photograph back into her bag, nodding. She's sorry too.

'Thanks anyway.'

She shuffles back out onto the street and looks around at the dimming town square. She really thought that this photograph – the one where Sharon looks like herself –

might jog some memories, might help her find out what happened, might get her somewhere – but she's exactly where she started; stuck at square one.

She turns the corner and walks along the side street, intending to start asking passing pedestrians, but her thoughts are veering off in wilder directions. Perhaps Sharon was never here that day at all. Perhaps Toby never brought her back to Rithling. Perhaps he took her somewhere else and is lying about it. She stops the train of thought dead, shaking her head.

It's not yet dark enough for the streetlamps to come on but the day is disappearing fast.

A patch of pavement ahead of her is lit with the dancing light from a flickering neon sign: Falcon Taxis. The others were adamant that Sharon intended to get a taxi back to Kedbury that day – in time for the Valentine Show. It is worth a try.

She walks inside and a bell mechanism clangs on the door behind her. When the man behind the counter looks up, she sees that beneath all the dark hair he is younger than she first thought, just a teenager.

'You need a taxi?'

'Er, no, I just, I just want to ask you something.'

The stack of newspapers on the counter rustles as he drops the magazine he was reading on to the pile – shiny pages about shiny inanimate objects, corners curled by the sweat of his grip. The aroma of some sort of food is drifting from somewhere. There is an adjoining room off to the left, but it is mostly hidden behind a beaded curtain.

'You want to book?'

'First, if you don't mind, I want to ask you' – she is reaching into her bag – 'if you'd have a look at this photograph… It's… She's…'

'This is a taxi company.'

The lad stops leaning on the counter and straightens up. He is as tall and broad as a man.

'Yes, I know, but can I just ask…'

Their eyes meet. His face is looking younger and less amenable by the second.

'Is there someone… Are you in charge here?' she asks falteringly.

She looks around. There are a couple of wonky-looking chairs crammed in by the window and a half-dead peace lily flopping on the ledge.

'I know what this is,' he says, ignoring her question. 'They already asked my dad about that woman. He's got nothing to do with it.'

The lad's tone seems almost aggressive.

'Okay, but is your dad here?'

'Fran!' he calls loudly through a doorway, and a slightly older, slightly taller brother appears.

Picking up on his brother's tone, he immediately folds his arms. Zoya turns to address him with the same question.

'Is your dad here?'

'No, he's out on a job,' the older brother explains.

'It's about that stupid woman who threw herself off the bridge,' the younger brother growls at his shoulder before staring at Zoya again. 'I've told you – Dad never saw her. It's got nothing to do with him.'

The older brother is wearing the same glowering expression. She knows they aren't going to look at her photograph.

'Like Lech says,' he states with finality. 'So, do you want a taxi – or do you want to leave?'

Zoya's eyes flicker from one brother to the other and then she turns and leaves. The street already feels darker, but a jagged grey gash of monochrome sunset is tearing through the sky, lighting the world in surreal contrasts.

Zoya walks a few streets to the outskirts and is as far as the lane before her heartbeat slows. She glances back at the town – the streetlamps are beginning to glow amber – then keeps on walking.

The road narrows as she presses onwards, uphill. The trees thicken and sway overhead. There are no pavements or streetlamps here. There's a chance she might miss dinner now but trudging through the shadows is better than waiting for a taxi with those boys.

***

The next morning finds Reed driving to the seaside with a smile on his face. A smooth road hushes his tyres and leads him along the top of the cliffs. Lush gardens line the approach road on one side; on the other, the sea, gently swelling in the bay.

The clifftop road broadens into a gentle turning circle in front of an inviting clean white building as the sun brightens unseasonably in the sky. Reed takes the van in a slow arc around the neatly planted shrubbery, pauses by the porch to read the elegant sign, then drives around the corner to the visitor's car park.

When he gets out, he can hear the waves synchronising like a choir, dotted with the caw of gulls, distant and muted and discrete.

Inside, he finds himself greeted warmly by a member of staff, as if the fancy retirement home was a classy hotel. He is expected, she tells him, and directs him to a smart, sea-view lounge to wait. George isn't here yet. The receptionist was going to telephone his room.

The view is framed by fine grasses rippling in a pleasant breeze. Reed can see the soft, sugary mounds of sandbanks dropping to a gingery beach. Old wooden break posts dot lines across the sand in comforting recession. He watches the sea as it glides in silvery sheets over the long, low shore.

After a few minutes, Reed decides he should probably take a seat. He folds himself into a plush grey armchair and notices that the pot plant to his side is real. He is still caressing the large variegated leaf when George walks in.

'Reed?' George says, spreading his arms in greeting as he strides through the arch.

His warm, confident voice makes the question sound more like an announcement and Reed finds himself rising from the chair.

He has never met George before but likes him immediately. His bright, inquisitive eyes are as captivating as his voice had been. When Reed telephoned, he had been pleasantly surprised; George immediately understood Reed's plan and welcomed his visit. George had even swapped some things around in his schedule to accommodate him – he seemed very busy for a retired septuagenarian: no sitting around watching daytime telly for him.

'George.'

Reed greets him in return and finds his hand being warmly shaken.

'I must say, I find your idea delightful – and I have just the thing.'

Reed smiles.

'Now' – George checks his shiny watch – 'I do have to be back by eleven for the games club, but I wonder if you might like to take in a walk first? We could still fit in a quick cuppa before I have to start. I've already fished it out ready for you – up in my room – so we have about an hour. What say you? Quick stroll to the point and back? I'm sure I have some stories you won't have heard yet. Be a shame for you to come all this way and not see the sea!'

Reed nods.

'George, I'd be honoured.'

CHAPTER 20

Okay, so this has happened. I didn't mean to drop off. It had got so quiet and so late and so dark that I must have fallen asleep, waiting. My neck feels sore from accidentally using the windowpane as a pillow. I give it a massage, wondering at the sensations – given that I am here and not here at the same time.

I get out of my car and stretch my legs. I look up and down the street just to check that I'm not really awake: no people, no cars, no animals.

I check the street outside Falcon Taxis. I don't think Mr Malish came back. But now I have an opportunity: I can go inside and have a look. That's what Reed would do.

'Oh that's another thing' – he once told me – *'we can open all doors.'*

I walk across the road and step into the small, bright office, my feet padding cautiously on the scuffed vinyl tiles. I look around for something locked to open – just to check.

I lean forward on the stubby counter, listening for sounds of the family beyond: nothing. I look all around the scruffy office, spying a small safe. I creep around the counter, noticing my light, timid steps. There's no reason for me to be scared.

I pull open the safe by its dial – a dial I didn't have to know the combination for. Inside, I see a petty-cash box, some papers… but nothing of interest. I close the safe, pleased to have confirmed my test.

Yes, I am all alone in the world.

There's a gap in the beaded curtain, where I can see an old lime sofa and a chunky television with a family photo on top. There's also a radio control station set up just inside the door. The wooden beads clack behind me as I slip through to investigate and are still swinging against my leg when I pick up the bookings ledger.

I flick the pages, trying to figure out if the dates are easy to read. I peer closer, looking for the night that Sharon died.

I half expect to find a page mysteriously ripped out, but there isn't one. Everything seems present and correct. I run my finger down the paper, transforming the wriggly biro letters into some system that makes sense. Names and times and destinations bob around and then I find her name – 'Sharon' – and the destination 'Kedbury' and a time.

The police must already have this information. Were the sons just lying about Mr Malish not having seen her that night? I trace my finger across the entry, pointing at each word like an accusation. 'No show' is written in capitals at the end of the row – but is that really what happened?

There's nothing concrete about two hastily scribbled words in a margin – they could have been added at any time.

***

Zoya jolts with the shock of being woken. There is the seamed, leather headrest and the banging of hands on the window and a wild rocking of the car. There are also jeering noises and harsh laughter and the faces of the two Malish lads. Lech is looking down into the car at her and pulling a mocking expression.

They laugh and walk away.

'Told you it was that bitch's car,' she hears the other one say, as they walk up the street in the direction of the cab office.

'Yeah, piece-of-shit car.'

Zoya waits until they have gone, catching her breath and watching the doorway warily. They are just teenage boys acting like teenage boys. She tells herself they will have forgotten about her already, moving their banter on to some other target of derision by now, probably talking drivel about their dream cars.

Zoya turns the key in the ignition and pulls into the empty road. She still wants to talk to Mr Malish – but not tonight.

***

The next day Zoya has skipped class again.

She didn't plan to ditch the class but overheard people talking about the 'accident' at breakfast and it made her want to get away. They were saying that people should just accept that horrible accidents happen sometimes and should stop being so 'conspiracy theory' about it. So, she followed her feet and left.

The dance studios, once warm, comforting cocoons for new, creative relationships, now feel stifling to her. She had to get out.

So here she is on a gravelly lane that slides up from the main road to a fence and a hidden rise. The turning isn't far from the ravine bridge and that had been her original destination, but she found herself veering away at the last minute, in search of some air. Finding the lane and the promise of soft sighs from the valley, she set off walking uphill.

She strides onwards, hoping for a private place beyond the gate where she can be reminded that there is still oxygen in her lungs. She wants to lift her face into the wild winds but there aren't any, just a dropping breeze and a day that hangs blankly overhead. She walks on, in search of air and space and sky.

This lane doesn't seem much used and the fields beyond look overgrown with ragged shrubs and patchy with boulders and stones. The high hills of the valley surround her with their rocky green walls.

The farmer's gate, when she finally gets to it, seems like it has been locked shut forever, the rusty padlock encrusted with dirt. There is a stile next to it which Zoya clambers onto. She has always had the impulse to climb, to follow paths, to place herself in the nooks and crannies of the physical world.

She pauses at the top of the stile, resting on the post. Looking upwards, she craves the sight of soaring birds, but finds none – only the muggy cover of a low-hanging, featureless sky.

She slips off the stile neatly, landing her feet on a dusty path that seems to fade into the grass. The way ahead looks rocky and scrubby – steeper and less appealing with every stride.

She spies a cluster of boulders and makes for it, finally sitting, short of breath, on a rock. She looks down the valley while her fingers stroke tufty mosses. There's a heaviness in her legs that a dancer shouldn't have.

From the rise, she can't see anything of the town. She can't see or hear the road, can't see another soul. Shadowy brushstrokes and inky cracks colour the hill slopes above her; unreachable angles dashed with fallen scree, frozen in time, forever slipping to the valley floor.

Her muddy boots scrape against the rock. She closes her eyes and listens to the snap of stalks in the waking wind. As the breeze picks up, the scent of rich, hard animal pellets reaches her nose. She opens her eyes again and her gaze drifts up to the sky.

She sees the sharp, speeding drop of a peregrine falcon darting like a bullet to the ground. Zoya knows she is lucky to have caught it, but the bird spot doesn't change her mood.

She feels in her bag for the figurine and looks at the ornament in her hand. Sharon bought her this but never got to give it to her. They found it among her things. There was a tag with a message already written, intended as a goodbye-and-thank-you present at the end of the year.

It's an owl.

Sharon had bought it for her because of their shared delight in all the charity shop tat, but the written note had been heartfelt and real.

She runs her fingers over it, needing to touch something that Sharon touched. She looks at it again. The owl's wings are outstretched as if in flight, but its feet are melded to a base of ceramic rocks so that the ornament can stand up on a mantlepiece or a coffee table or a kitchen shelf. Why an owl, Zoya wonders, a fellow night-adventurer? There's so much that Sharon never knew about her and Zoya can never tell her now.

She puts the figurine safely away in her bag.

She is exhausted with the racing cycle of thoughts and questions and suspicions that have now taken up a permanent position in her head and tries to lose herself in the solidity of the land. She moves her hand over the knobbly surface of the rock, trying to imagine the ancient glacier that once swept along the valley and deposited it there.

She looks closer at the speckled surface and sees something that could be a stain. Stone stained with darkness. It could be anything – from rabbit guts to ancient sheep shit – but the stain gathers her worry, like a vortex. She doesn't need the paranoia. She jumps up and backs away.

She walks back down the hill and over the stile and onto the gravel. From this angle, she spots a set of deeply gouged car tracks that she hadn't noticed before. The tracks make Zoya picture scenes of frantic chase – a dark, desperate scramble over the gate stuck with time and into the nothingness of the night.

***

Reed walks into the street, secretly impressed by the formal charm of the buildings rising on either side. He has never really noticed the bright-bricked smartness of Nottingham before. It isn't what he was expecting when he talked to Jane about it over the phone, imagining her in a tiny, glass box of an apartment, stacked one on top of another with other young professionals; tiny kitchens made for one.

He recognised her accent though: a native of Shilly-on-Sea.

He checks the address and scans the tiers of brick and stone. It doesn't look as if anyone – anyone at all – is home. He finds the right door and buzzes the intercom.

'Hi, this is Reed. We spoke on the phone…' He's still not sure how to describe his quest. 'I hope it's still okay?'

The fuzzy voice sounds loud by his ear.

'Yes, yes. No problem. Come right on up!'

CHAPTER 21

Zoya is sitting in the Rithling Arms by the tall window that overlooks the square and the looming hills and glowering sky. Her chin rests in her cupped palms, the soft wool of the sleeves she has pulled over her hands caressing the skin of her cheeks. The conversation of the few customers at the other side of the bar is so low in the mix that it doesn't interrupt her thoughts. Her glass of wine has barely been touched.

As she looks through the tall window, the scratches on the glass vanish and she is transported to the hills beyond the town. In contrast to her still, lost-in-thought pose, her eyes are dancing, searching for meaning in the landscape. The jagged line of the crest becomes an erratic heartbeat, a musical composition, a crumbling scone broken in two.

She usually sits in the main bar, concertina-squeezed on the bench with friends, but today she sits alone and watches the afternoon and thinks.

Jo and Sandy have started working on an extra piece together. Clare is entering a street dance competition. Ivan is applying for a scholarship. Or so she hears. Everyone else seems to be getting on with things but Zoya feels like she has wandered from the trail and might never be able to get back on that path of classes and rehearsals and being passionate about dance.

She looks up to the thickening skies and imagines soaring up there, away from the deep, sharp cut of the rocky river below and beyond the valley and away. She imagines flying over the fields and the country roads and beyond Kedbury. Over the forests and cottages and towns and motorways; over the cows and sheep and stripes of agriculture; over the streams and rivers and canals; pressing on toward the coastline and the glittering sea's edge. She imagines swooping and gliding over the long beach and the reed-prickled dunes and the bright café at the corner, lifted by sun-warmed water on winds that carry her to the top of the hill and the house with a whale on the roof.

Richard and Abigail are setting sail today. She hasn't seen them since Christmas and hasn't told them anything about Sharon or the bridge. She had planned to insist on staying on at the dance school, to argue that it's better to stay with friends who are all supporting each other through the same grief. It might be true about the support and the grief – for the others – but *Zoya* wouldn't know. In the end, the days stretched on and she didn't tell her dad and aunt anything at all.

The clock on the town hall chimes three o'clock. They will be sailing by now. She imagines their ship slipping further out to sea on blue, shining waves, heading toward the sparkling Mediterranean and the sun and further away from her. She conjures a bird's-eye view of their relative positions – she, landlocked and earth-tied; her family, gliding on water toward new experiences and a bright horizon, and away, away…

She thinks of the auditions and the phone call and everyone sharing champagne; and of the bag-packing and driving through the lanes and seeing the school for the first time. She mentally flips through a catalogue of memories: of meeting Sandy and Tilda and Lauren, of Leon giving her his T-shirt, of Sharon swapping rooms. She thinks of the daily digests and the Friday trips into town and of discovering her rooftop for the first time. She thinks of the tree-tops and the timetables and of giant scones cut in two. She thinks of the theatre wings and the hushed audience and the spotlit applause. All this is behind her and she doesn't know what is ahead.

The young barman in the striped T-shirt passes her table, collecting empty glasses from the otherwise deserted room.

'Are you alright?'

She looks up at him, automatically dabbing at her eyes in case she has been crying but they remain tired and dry.

The barman picks up another used pint glass, placing it in his stack with a satisfying clink. He smiles at her, revealing the tooth gap she has noticed before.

'Can I ask you something?' she ventures.

'Yes,' he replies, coming to a rest, the glasses at one hip.

She pulls out her photograph of Sharon.

'Do you recognise her?'

She passes it to his outstretched hand, accidentally grazing his fingers with hers. His skin is warm, like his smile.

She watches him looking at the photograph, his brows knotted hard with concentration. He seems to be really, properly looking, unlike some of the others she has stopped to ask.

'I don't think I recognise her... But that doesn't mean she hasn't been in. You at the dance school?'

He hands it back to her but remains where he stands, open to more conversation.

Zoya nods.

'Okay, thanks. She might have been here with someone else... with a man who... with someone sort of...' Zoya thinks for a moment before rephrasing it. 'With a... bad man...?'

As soon as the words leave her mouth, she feels foolish but there is nothing to worry about. The barman seems to have picked up on her reaction to her own phrasing and they share a look.

'I'm thinking specifically of Saturday, the fifteenth of February.'

'Valentine's weekend? Well, as it happens, I do remember clocking a couple in here and thinking it must be the worst date in history.'

Zoya straightens up.

'I remember because most people who come in here are usually locals and you lot from the dance school – and this pair seemed different, not ramblers either – not at all. Tell you who was here that day: that Luke who works at your place – sometimes pops in for a soft drink. Anyway, they didn't seem to know him so... or maybe he left before they came in. Can't remember.'

'Okay, so, tell me about this man.'

'Yes, he was with a woman, I couldn't tell you who, though, I just remember him making her stump up a tenner for the drinks and not even giving her the change... that's when I realised he was a dick.'

The barman perches on the arm of a chair, arms folded around the stack of glasses.

'I had noticed him come in, though, because he was shouting out of the doorway to some kids who were hanging about his car. I had a quick look: those Malish lads – I suppose they love cars – were taking an interest in it because it was some unusual looking kind of thing. Um... an orange Capri, I think. I don't really give a shit about cars myself. Um...'

'So, he was a shouty man with an unusual car...?'

'At first, he seemed kind of... charming? Charming smile... I don't know – blokes really aren't my type – but after being a bit of a dick to his girlfriend at the bar, I kept clocking them. They sat right over there.' He points out a table in the main room of the pub. 'It wasn't that they were arguing, just, I don't know, a tense discussion. I couldn't hear – it just seemed nasty from where I was standing. Anyway, I don't think they left together, and I remember being glad about that.'

'So, what did he look like?'

'Erm... do you have a photograph I can look at?'

'No, I don't. Not of him. Do you remember what *he* looked like… please?'

The barman sets down his stack of glasses and rests his head in his hands, massaging his temples and ruffling his sandy hair a little, trying to think. He jerks his head up and makes eye contact with Zoya, snapping his fingers.

'Okay, yes. He was definitely taller than average, not like big and burly, thinner than me' – the barman absent-mindedly touches his own small, soft belly, as he thinks – 'but… shoulders…'

He gestures a straight line to illustrate.

'You know what he was, he was the type of guy who takes up a lot of room with his gestures, you know what I mean? Rangy. Um… brown, wavy hair… I think…' – he nods in conclusion – 'yeah.'

He looks at her with a hopeful little smile.

'Thanks,' she says, impressed with his observational skills.

'Okay.'

He stands and moves away.

'What's your name?' Zoya asks.

He pauses.

'Zach.'

'Thanks, I'm Zoya. So' – he turns back again – 'so what happened, where did he go? When did his… friend leave? When did *he*?'

'It must have been after we got busy, around, I don't know, early evening… I'll get Mum.'

Zoya feels like springing up and following but remains at the table where she sits alone for a couple of minutes, tapping a fingernail on the tabletop.

When Zach reappears with a woman, Zoya recognises her as the landlady and smiles her friendliest smile. She can see now that she and Zach are related – the same pale, grey-blue eyes. This must be the same Lynn Jones whose name is above the door.

Lynn sits down at the table.

'Who is it you're looking for?'

Zach interjects.

'You were here on Valentine's weekend, weren't you, Mum?'

'No, I was out on a date with Brad Pitt.' She winks at Zoya. 'Yes.'

'There was a man and woman – not regulars – came in late afternoon – he was shouting about his car... maybe you remember?'

She shakes her head.

'No, but I do remember there was a woman here then. I thought she was one of you dance lot – but she wasn't with the usual crowd so... anyway, I heard her ordering a taxi in the hall there.'

The landlady nods to the hallway behind the bar that leads to the toilets.

'When she hung up, I pointed out the fire escape – just there off the hallway, said she could go out to her taxi from there.'

'Why?' Zoya asks.

'I don't know, something in the tone of her voice that I picked up on. You can't run pubs in Sheffield for twenty years without developing a sixth sense for this kind of thing. Us women need to stick together, you know.'

Zoya nods slowly, thinking it through. If it *was* Sharon, then she had left the pub alone and safe. Her brow furrows slightly.

'So, what about the man?'

Lynn shrugs.

'I honestly don't remember him. Sorry, love. Are these friends of yours?'

The landlady stands up from the table and Zoya feels panicked by the approaching end of the conversation but doesn't know what else to ask.

'The last I saw of that man I described,' Zach adds, 'he was standing just outside and shouting something – maybe at those lads? I remember thinking he might start causing trouble, but he never came back in.'

Zoya remembers what she read in the taxi book.

'Was this around six, do you think?'

'Could have been.'

Lynn has gone back to work and Zach makes to follow her. Then he pauses again and turns.

'Is this about that death at the bridge I read about?'

Zoya nods.

'So, why aren't the police asking all these questions…?' he asks, adopting an expression of genuine curiosity.

Zoya looks away again, aiming to divert her swelling, angry tears.

'I don't know.'

***

Reed blinks back the tears that formed when the wire-haired pointer winded him and looks down at the happy mutt that is currently giving him all of his doggy love.

'Wolfy!' comes the chastising voice from the doorway.

When Reed looks along the drive toward the speaker, he finds a young mother in a bright cardigan with an amused smile.

'No harm done,' Reed says.

'How tall are you?'

When Reed looks down at the source of the voice, he finds a small boy standing at his thigh.

'Er...'

The dog hops down to the ground again and starts circling him, wagging his tail.

'How old are you?' comes the little voice again.

'I'm sorry about all this,' the woman says. 'Are you Reed?'

He approaches her, trying to avoid the excitable dog weaving around his legs.

'Yes, I...'

'Jack, come here please,' Issy says, holding out one hand to her son while grabbing for Wolfy's collar with the other. 'Come on in. Please consider this a warm, northern welcome!'

'Thanks, I...'

She smiles, gesturing with just her shoulders because both hands are now full.

'Welcome to Leeds!'

***

After the pub, Zoya knew exactly where to go. She is becoming familiar with the side street and the taxi office and makes her way there, looking at the pavement pensively, as if she might find a trail of clues. She almost bumps into someone whose feet appear suddenly before her and looks up to find Mr Malish walking the other way.

She stops dead, having found her target, and he does the same in reaction. He wears an unsettled expression, not knowing what to make of her strange determined recognition, and not knowing who she is.

Then his face darkens as the cogs in his mind begin to turn.

'You the girl my sons told me about?' he demands with a slight accent, but seems more fearful and less intimidating than either of them.

She almost feels bad having interrupted him and doesn't want to spoil his day.

'Mr Malish, can I ask you a question please?'

'No, no, I don't know what you mean.'

Mr Malish turns and walks back again, back in the direction of the taxi office. Zoya follows, daring to lay a hand on his coat sleeve.

'Please, please, Mr Malish. I need your help.'

The beseeching tone perhaps stirs some sense of chivalry in him, and he lets her stop his walking. They turn to one another at the corner of the street.

He raises his hands in a gesture of innocence and begins to ramble, talking low and quick.

'No, no, I never saw that woman they are all asking about. I don't know what you mean. I'm sorry. I'm sorry,' he says, and then carries on walking up the street.

Zoya follows him, scrabbling in her bag pocket for the photograph. Then she races ahead to hold it up in front of his face.

She notices his eyes restlessly wandering all around the picture; it seems obvious that he doesn't want to look.

'Please, please, Mr Malish, please, just take a look.'

She notices his Adam's apple bobbing as he readies himself to look at the photograph.

'This is my friend, Sharon – she liked dancing and daisies and going clubbing. And strawberry jam. She ordered a taxi from here to Kedbury on the fifteenth of February. We were doing a performance at the theatre there. She was really excited. We all were. But she never turned up.'

She watches his dark eyes regarding Sharon in the photograph. Perhaps they even seem to be getting moist.

Then he looks down at his feet and his shoulders begin to shake.

***

Zoya and Mr Malish are sitting in her Suzuki in the car park. The police station is looming close by, its windows quietly staring across the square.

Zoya places her hand on his arm and gives him a tissue. He wipes his eyes and shakes his head, as if to shake away the emotion.

'So, you told the police that Sharon's booking was a no show?' Zoya asks gently, prompting him to elaborate on what he was saying between sobs.

'Okay.' He takes a breath to calm himself. 'Okay, I'll tell you.'

He looks her in the eye.

'I did pick her up from the pub there. She was going to Kedbury, yes.'

'But... she never got there, did she...?'

Zoya is hanging on his every word, desperate to find out but not wanting to scare him away. She doesn't feel like she's in a car with a killer.

'No.'

He looks away again, down at the wrinkled tissue in his hands. He looks like a man hanging his head in shame.

'Okay, she said she had no money for the fare and asked me to stop at the cashpoint. So, we stop at that small supermarket, Savertown – you know the one just out of town? She gets out and uses the cashpoint and it's taking a long, long time. She keeps trying and keeps putting her card in again. So, I call to her, out of the window, "What's wrong?"...'

'You left her because she had no money…?' Zoya asks, jumping in, barely masking her anger.

'I… yes, but it was only there, not really even out of the town. You know, I have two sons to raise. No mother. She died when they were young. We… I… have bills to pay… It's not a free service we provide. I didn't know anything would happen to her… How could I know?'

He starts shaking his head again.

'No, no, you couldn't know,' Zoya says, as he reaches for the door handle to open it and go.

He pauses, as if to speak again, but closes his mouth and gets out of the car.

'Please, please, Mr Malish…' Zoya begins to speak but he closes the passenger door.

She gets out and rushes after him.

'Please! Please! Mr Malish…'

He looks around nervously and hurries away across the car park.

'Hey, Dad!'

There they are, the two sons, strutting along the top side of the square. They have seen Zoya following their father and make an abrupt turn in her direction.

'Please, Mr Malish,' Zoya calls, louder and more desperately. 'Did you see anyone with an orange Capri? That night, Mr Malish…?'

He might be out of earshot and, in any case, doesn't turn around.

'What have we told you?' asks the younger son, Lech.

Zoya watches Mr Malish striding on past them, away from her and from his confession and out of the sight line of the police station. He isn't going to come back and talk to her.

The sons stand, arms folded, in her path. This is pointless.

Zoya heads back to her car, shuts and locks the door behind her, buckles her seat belt and starts the engine. The sons turn and strut away, too young to know much about anything, too big to be ignored.

Zoya drives out of the car park and turns, not toward the dance school, but toward the small supermarket out of town.

APRIL

....

Reed drives through the suburbs slowly, seeing house after blocky stone house. The grey slate roofs and grey walls and grey pavements are separated by jade box bushes and thin railings. Knobbly beech trees flank the road. He finds the street, if not the house, and decides to park where he can.

Stepping out onto the pavement, he feels that the air has a nip. It seems that Aprils in Aberdeen are cold. The wind tugs his hair sharply and he decides to make a move.

He finds the house in question. It doesn't look studenty at all. He knocks on the door.

A young, burly man in a scruffy sweater answers, probably a postgrad.

'Yeah?' he says in a posh accent.

'Is, er, Cal, here?'

Reed feels awkward using such a casual name for someone he has never actually met.

'Cally? Sure.'

***

An orange Ford Capri is parked outside the multiplex in Kedbury. A tall, wavy-haired man is crouching by the rear wheel, scrutinising the panel. He seems satisfied by his inspection and his angry expression subsides. He stands and steps back a few paces to admire the overall shape of his vehicle and his mouth takes on the hook of a small, smug smile.

'Have you had a prang, mister?'

The tall man turns around to see a couple of lads sitting smoking on a low wall. Their postures make them seem younger than they are – like little kids swinging their legs above the pavement – but the size of their feet tells a different story.

The Capri owner looks at them and cocks his head slightly. They might be taking an aspirational interest, or they might be taking the piss. His eyes flit over the sight of them and he decides to indulge them in a spot of conversation.

'No, some idiot just got too close. Hasn't scratched her, luckily.'

'It's in good condition,' Fran says.

'Oh, you know something about cars?'

Fran shrugs.

'How much?' Lech asks, and Alex jerks his gaze toward him.

He laughs. He's not about to talk finances with some kids.

'How much did you get it for?' Lech repeats, but doesn't get an answer. 'Give you fifty quid,' he adds, and the brothers snicker.

'*Would* you ever sell it?' Lech asks, interested, trying to seem more adult, all traces of snickering gone.

The man looks again at the long sleek lines of the bodywork, smiling, and looks back at them, slowly shaking his head.

'We saw you in Rithling, didn't we?'

The man's smile evaporates, and he turns toward them, mulling over an idea.

'Are you lads local, then?'

They look at him, waiting to hear the question seemingly brewing in his mind.

'Maybe you can help me out?'

The man's face brightens into a charming smile, but his voice sounds bashful as his faltering sentences build.

The sons can't help feeling that they are being called upon somehow, drawn into the cool Capri owner's confidence, honoured with his trust. They stop swinging their feet.

'A friend of mine goes to some dance school near there – have you heard of it? They're keeping something of mine for me and I've been meaning to stop by and collect it – but I can't remember where it is. I must have lost the address...'

The man looks at his feet, acting like someone embarrassed by his own stupidity, then looks up at them with bright, hopeful eyes.

'A dance school?' Lech asks incredulously, as if he doubts that such a thing exists.

'Yeah,' Fran chimes in. 'Yeah we sometimes get jobs up there – my dad does, he's a taxi driver.' He turns to look at his brother whose face shows it is all news to him.

'It's up by the back lanes somewhere,' he explains. Then he looks back at the smiling man. 'Must be on the map, though?'

The man nods with the smallest of movements.

'Hey, I wonder, would you like a spin in the old thing?' he gestures at the Capri.

The younger lad looks like he is contemplating it, whereas the older brother is processing some different thoughts instead.

'There's a woman looking for you, been asking about your car,' Fran says, blurting out his realisation without a second thought.

'Is that your friend? With the thing?' asks Lech.

'What does she look like?' Alex asks, as if trying to figure out whether they mean the same person.

Lech shrugs again.

'I don't know. She's like the only black girl in the town.'

'No, she's…'

'Something, though – hardly snow white, is she?'

Alex smiles.

'Yeah, that's her.'

After a long, cool, stare into the middle distance, Alex breaks into a warm smile and paces toward the passenger door.

'So, you fancy a spin?'

A car horn beeps, and the lads' eyes jerk toward it. They see their dad's taxi parked down the street and quickly, guiltily, stub out their fag ends and toss them over the wall. They can see him watching through the open window. He looks worried.

One after the other, they hop off the wall and onto the pavement, sloping off toward the taxi, their voices low and humble now and talking over one another.

'That's our dad.'

'Thanks, but got to go...'

Alex leans lightly on the car roof, his fingers moving gently over the paintwork, caressing it. He watches the Toyota Corolla pull away while a cold expression settles, like snowfall, on his face.

****

Zoya is alone again in the pub. This time she is sitting at the small round table for two that Zach pointed out to her. She is looking at the stippled surface of the copper and worrying at it with her fingers.

She looks up and out of the window, adjusting her eyes to peer into the gloomy evening enveloping the town square. There is a dark figure out there, sitting quietly on the wall of the car park. He is facing the other way, but she recognises the coat.

Zoya finds herself rising from her seat to get a better look and then drifting outside, crossing the quiet street and approaching him.

He seems to be sitting watching the police station, which stands quietly at the bottom of the square.

'Hi,' she ventures, softly.

Mr Malish looks around. His eyes are wide and dark. His look of recognition, she notices, is shot through with relief and compassion and fear.

Zoya steps over the low wall and stands before him. She opens her hand.

'Come on,' she says, gently.

They grab wrists as he allows her to help him stand.

They walk silently down through the car park. At the entrance to the police station, Mr Malish pauses, his feet shuffling. He raises his head in Zoya's direction, but his eyes dash all over the square – looking everywhere but at her face.

'Do you know what you're going to say?' Zoya asks gently.

Mr Malish looks at his feet and nods.

She watches him unblinkingly, not wanting to scare him off with questions but desperate to know all the same. He must see her desperation and clears his throat slightly.

'The thing is' – a pained smile appears briefly – 'I did see your friend later that night... I...' He licks his lips and clears his throat again. 'I was driving back from a job that took me to Kedbury and I'd just passed the bridge – I like that route, it's quieter...'

Zoya watches him, unmoving, her eyes steady and un-blinking and clear.

Mr Malish looks away.

'I saw her getting into a car.'

His words dry up. Zoya gently takes his arm.

'Did you get the registration number?'

He shakes his head. *No, why would he?* she thinks.

'Do you remember the make and model?' she asks.

He looks at her and nods.

***

Within five minutes of Mr Malish disappearing inside the police station, Zoya is back at her table in the pub. The same glass of wine is sitting in front of her and none of the locals littering the place seem to have noticed she was ever gone. Through the window, she keeps an eye on the distant police station.

Lynn, the landlady, sweeps by and smiles at her.

'A friend of yours was asking after you,' she says.

A half smile involuntarily breaks out on Zoya's face and her mood leaps.

'Oh?'

'Tall, thin…'

'Pale looking…?' Zoya's smile spreads. She could really do with an old friend. 'Reddish hair?'

Lynn's brow furrows slightly.

'No, not red…'

'Who was it?'

'Sorry, love, he didn't say. I didn't recognise him.'

Zoya's attention is drawn to the male presence standing above her – Zach with a stack of clean ashtrays and a serious expression.

'*I* did…' he says.

***

Inside the interview room, Mr Malish is hunched over a polystyrene cup of weak tea.

'And can you tell us what type of car it was?' the detective asks.

Mr Malish swallows, intending his words to be helpful and clear.

'It was a Ford Capri, very distinctive.'

'And could you tell the colour of the car, Mr Malish?'

'It was dark, but I would say it was orange.' He thinks back to picking up his sons in Kedbury and seeing it again. 'Yes, definitely orange.'

***

Later, in the deep darkness of the lonely rural night, the wind whips along the valley, cutting between the hills. Grasses lash the hidden hillside, strobing in the flickering, crackling light of flames. Thick, black sheets of toxic smoke billow up into the pitch darkness as the fuming fire blazes on. The roaring flames rage, witnessed by nobody, as an orange Ford Capri burns and blackens and burns.

CHAPTER 23

The taxi glides around a leafy corner and the headlights illuminate the thick curve of trees. Leaves fan beside them, emerging from the darkness as prickling, sharp-cut shadows that ripple coal to ash to chalk in the light of the car. Then they are swallowed again by the peaty, black, left-behind night.

The stiff seams of the leather seat feel like chains beneath Zoya's skin as she runs her fingertip back and forth, back and forth, back and forth.

'It's just around here on the left.'

The sweeping beam of light picks out for a second the tiny wooden sign hidden in the overgrown foliage, only ever noticed by people who already know that it is there. Jo Malish slows the vehicle, looking into the shadows for the easy-to-miss drive.

Zoya leans forward, her cheek by his headrest, scanning the dark, leafy shadows, aiming to help him out. Although this is a lift, not a paid fare, she is sitting in the back seat. They have barely spoken throughout the journey – a pair of strange allies, not friends.

She saw him coming out of the police station and lingered at the corner where he confirmed his statement to her with a nod and shining eyes.

It's not that far from the town to the dance school, if you know which turns to make, but the drive seemed long and silent, neither one of them wanting to speak or knowing what to say.

Zoya feels glad that Mr Malish saw Sharon and relieved he has told the police and encouraged that they can add one more event to their timeline – but none of it lifts her spirits. She feels empathy for Mr Malish, having carried his guilt-sodden secret, and respect that he has now done the right thing, but still she blames him: if he hadn't abandoned Sharon at the roadside, wouldn't she still be alive today?

The Corolla makes the turn and trundles up the long, dark drive. The main building appears from the darkness across the broad sweep of swaying grass, glinting angularly with moonlight like a jewel.

The tyres sound on the gravel as they get closer, mimicking the low rumblings of anxiety she is feeling inside. What will happen with the police investigation now? Does she really want to know what exactly happened – what Sharon felt and suffered – just before she died?

The taxi stops and Zoya gets out, closing the passenger door with a gentle thud. She pauses at the driver's window to find him looking up at her.

'Thank you,' she says, holding his gaze.

Eventually, he nods.

She hears the retreat of the vehicle behind her as she walks to the main entrance, fiddling in her bag for the key. It's not that late, really, and there will be lights on around the back in the residential blocks, but here, everything is dark and dead.

She raises her key to the keyhole but finds the door unlocked. She walks inside.

Moonlit and shadowed, the atrium looks just like that tiny-captioned black-and-white photo from the history book and just as indistinct. Her eyes can hardly separate the pillars from the spidery canteen furniture from the tilted shadows falling from the light fittings and bannisters. The twisting staircase cuts black shapes into the floor.

The deserted atrium seems to creak with age, noises indistinguishable from the moaning wind in the twisted trees or the menacing tread of feet on the stair. She sees a shadow moving across the floor; the figure of someone almost silent in the dark above her.

Her head jerks around to look up at him. Her breath catches and her soles squeak on the floor.

The man walks down toward her, silhouette looming closer against the night's sky.

'It's just me, Zoya.'

She thinks she hears those words, but the voice seems muffled by her beating heart and crowded by all sorts of imaginings. She can't move her feet.

'I just got back myself, I...' he says, the voice not familiar yet.

Then his face comes into focus and Zoya's shock is replaced by surprise.

Leon is standing before her, casually descending the last couple of steps.

She laughs out loud – *too* loudly; relief and happiness and comfort found in a friendly face.

'Leon! Good to see you!' she says, finding herself with her arms around him, burying her face in a hug that smells like the purple, *Liberte!* T-shirt he gave her.

They look at each other, smiling in the moonlight, and then he dips to pick up his bag.

They begin walking to the back corridors, their syncing footsteps making a comforting sound on the floor. She is thinking how to word her question about him coming back, but instead just slips her arm through his. It feels warm and strong.

They pass through a fire door into the studio block and find the lighting on.

'So, Zoya, how's the routine?' he asks, as they pass the doors to Studio 1.

They stroll in rhythm along the corridor.

'Developing,' she answers. 'They've given me the closing piece in the Midsummer Show.'

Hearing the words coming out of her mouth, she realises that she hasn't worked on it in days.

Leon's eyebrows rise as he nods slowly, looking suitably impressed.

'Got any ideas?' he asks.

'A few,' she replies, nodding herself.

'Show me?' Leon suggests.

Zoya looks at him and smiles.

'Tomorrow,' she agrees, nodding.

***

The next day, they are up on the flat roof and Zoya is showing Leon her routine. He is leaning against the wall, watching critically, professionally, and it feels just like old times.

Just as he is about to speak, giving her a note about the dance piece, she interrupts him.

'I'm glad you're back,' she tells him. 'I don't think anyone likes me anymore.'

'I don't think they like me either,' he says, evidently thinking about his absence and return.

'Nonsense. You're family,' she replies, pulling a dismissive expression and pacing to keep her legs warm. 'You'll fit right back in.' She stops walking and pauses, a thought on the end of her tongue. 'Can I ask you something?'

Leon looks at his feet and sighs audibly.

'Yes, I went to the audition. No, I didn't get the part,' he says, reciting the words with resignation.

'Not that. It's just, I was thinking… I'd like a support – for the closing section of my routine. You know, so I can change that whole bit into a lift – but without making the whole thing a pas de deux…'

'I think that's a great idea.' Leon is smiling. 'Haven't you asked anyone yet?'

Zoya shakes her head. It occurs to her that there are some people she hasn't once spoken to, ever since Sharon's death.

'Would you?'

'Sure.'

His eyes look warm and glinting.

'The only thing is… it's my dance, still,' Zoya says. '*My* dance.'

'I know. Hey, why don't I dress "invisible" – all black, my head too. They've got these amazing costumes now, that puppeteers wear…'

'I've seen them! Or… *haven't* seen them.'

'So, it would be like… I just come in from nowhere and lift you like I'm not even there and then I can disappear again. And we work it with the lighting…'

'Yeah!'

'Yeah! That could be awesome.'

'Okay, so, after I do this' – Zoya begins to move – 'then I think we could work the lift in here.' She is gesturing her idea and marking out the choreography. 'I thought we could start it like' – she takes his arms and places his hands in position on her hips – 'this.'

They explore the move, testing out her idea.

'Yes, so how do you think we should go from here? Is it better to go down this way or turn into this…?'

'I thought this was *your* choreography?'

'Listen,' Zoya begins, her feet now firmly back on the floor. 'The way a man can tell the difference – whether he's helping or taking over – is really simple: was he asked or not?' She smiles. 'I asked.'

Suddenly, the door opens, and Luke is standing there with a worried look on his face.

'Leon, glad I found you. Listen, do you mind going with Olivia to the hospital? It's not good news about her sister. I don't think she's got long left. I'd go but I've got to collect the street dancers from Kedbury so I'm going to call a taxi for her and…'

'I'll take her,' Zoya interrupts. 'I'll take her in my car.'

CHAPTER 24

Zoya and Olivia are in the Suzuki, worried looks etched on both their faces. At the gates, she turns, not right toward Rithling, but left, heading for Leaton and the hospital and the sister with hours to live.

They aren't talking because what, really, is there to say?

The afternoon sky soon becomes blocked by the heavy overhang of trees, only making brief appearances above them, blue and pale and innocent, every now and then.

'Is this the quickest way?' Olivia asks in a small, urgent voice.

Zoya looks at her, adopts a comforting expression and nods.

'It might seem the long way round, going by the lanes, but it's actually shorter as the crow flies and we're not going to get snarled up in any traffic so' – she nods reassuringly again – 'we'll be there soon.'

She puts her foot down and zips along the quiet roads, maintaining a steady, confident path, no sudden swerves.

She drives on, pleased to see a road sign pointing to Leaton – not because she doubted the route but because it should reassure Olivia as best it can. But, when she sneaks a look at her passenger, Zoya's not sure she's even aware of the journey. She sees her staring blankly, thoughts – understandably – elsewhere.

The road ahead straightens and becomes flanked by very tall, thick trees, no sunny exit yet visible at the end. The Suzuki presses onwards, entering the dark, fluttering tunnel, and Zoya's eyes adjust.

A few moments later, there is a thud.

'What was that?' Olivia asks, her eyes widening.

Zoya checks the dashboard and senses for anything that feels off with the handling. Nothing seems to be wrong. Olivia is craning her neck, looking in the rear-view mirror, squinting to see the road they are leaving behind.

'Probably just a fox,' Zoya says, screwing up her face disdainfully, unable to make out anything on the shadowy receding lane. 'We can't stop; it's probably nothing, doesn't matter.'

She carries on driving and they don't say another word. Inside, Zoya feels sick and ashamed. There is something more important that they have to do now than go back to stop and check, but Zoya would hate to have hurt or injured any animal and worries all the same. That's all she can see now in her imagination – bloodied fur and lolling jaw.

***

Hours later, the Suzuki stands motionless, parked near the hospital on a stubby dead end of a side street with no houses, lit by old, faint streetlamps, and discovered after something of a search. The pavement opposite leads to a green mesh gateway. Boys in muddied football kits spill out from the gate, scuffing their way toward the main street with tired legs.

Two teenagers pause, looking at the car.

'No fucking way,' says the younger one, a mischievous glint lighting his eye.

'That fucking bitch,' concurs Fran, looking up and down the street.

No nosey neighbour windows, no cameras.

The clang of the mesh gate makes his head jerk. The team coach is locking up now, the last to leave. Lech just stands there, but Fran drops to his knee to tie a shoelace that doesn't need tying.

'Night, Mr Johnson,' he calls respectfully.

'Night, lads. See you next week.'

Mr Johnson jogs off around the corner, his sports bag bouncing as he goes. The brothers look again at one another then advance nonchalantly toward the car.

***

After a long, dark day hanging around the hospital, Zoya is staring at the long, dark road ahead. Olivia is with her family now and her sister, Bronwyn, is dead. With chronic illness and years of suffering, it is the compassionate sentiment that at least the deceased is 'at peace now' – but Zoya can't see anything peaceful in someone starving themselves to death.

She thought these thoughts earlier, while waiting at the hospital and trying to stay out of the way. On the surface, it seems as though Bronwyn did this to herself, but that's not the truth of it. Society did this to her. She was twenty-two. Zoya changes gear, grips the wheel harder and frowns, too angry for tears.

A lone car passes in the other direction and, once clear, Zoya flicks her headlamps back to full beam and charges ahead into the leaf-smothered darkness. She just wants to get home now, or to the nearest thing she's got.

Later on, the car feels odd; it slows and there's a funny noise. She sets her hazards blinking, finds the torch in the glove compartment and gets out to have a look.

From the tarmac, it's immediately obvious: the front tyre is flat.

'Fucking hell!' she shouts into the darkness.

This is the last thing she needs. Yes, she's got a torch and a spare and a jack in the back, but she really cannot be bothered with this *now*. If another car comes and they offer her a lift, she will get in and go wherever they take her.

She stands glumly in the quiet lane, the orange lights flashing across her skin. The night settles around her. She hears flapping, moaning, wood-pigeony sounds but no traffic. She wonders how long it would take to walk back to Leaton.

She goes to the boot of the car, intent on fishing out her *A–Z*. She's not sure exactly how far she's come already but, if she walks back to the junction, there might be a sign or a clue about where she is. And maybe more passing cars.

Then she sees it. One of the back tyres is also sagging. The shock realisation of malicious sabotage drops over her like an icy sheet of water and she is angry all over again.

She slams the boot shut and starts walking along the road.

The junction appears eventually, moonlit but offering no real clues. She peers along the roads, looking for a hint of a payphone or a house or a village. Nothing. It is hard to peer into the rural darkness. The dusty fields here seem to suck the light of the moon into the earth. It isn't like the nights back home, where the starlight shimmers over the sea.

One thing she *can* see though, beyond a sweep of shadowy fields, are the distant lights of Leaton; much further away than she had thought.

She looks back to her car, the hazard lights still twinkling in the leafy lane. If she is halfway between Leaton and the dance school, she may as well just walk back to the school. She turns again and starts marching in the original direction.

She is young and strong and her feet can take her anywhere she needs to go.

***

Barely fifteen minutes into her walk, Zoya hears a noise. Yes, there are beams of light growing in the darkness ahead of her. She doesn't get out of the way. There's always a chance that the driver won't see her and stop. She doesn't want to get run over, but she also doesn't want to miss out on a lift.

The road ahead seems straight enough, so she stands bravely in the middle of the tarmac and starts waving her arms. The car begins to slow, trundling toward her now at a pedestrian pace. She shields her eyes from the beams before the driver thoughtfully drops them. It looks like a Ford Fiesta. Zoya steps around to the driver's side and finds a youngish man looking at her with a friendly smile.

'Are you stranded?' he ask, pleasantly.

'I… er…'

There's just something about the way he's looking at her that makes her sentence drift away. Is it that they know each other, and she is failing to place him? His eyes do seem to register a look of recognition but no, she has never met him before.

She glances inside the car as far as possible, but you can't tell how tall someone is – how 'rangy' – when they are sitting down. What colour is his hair in daylight, she wonders, glancing at it surreptitiously.

They are looking at one another too closely and for too long.

'I'm, er…' Zoya begins, trying to make a decision. 'I'm… er… waiting for someone. They're on their way – to help me with my car.' She gestures back the way she has come. 'I thought you were someone else,' she adds and smiles politely.

He mirrors that smile back at her.

'So, let me give you a lift?' he says, the polite smile now spreading wide.

Is that a smile you would describe as 'charming', she wonders? He doesn't seem that sure of himself.

'Sorry, I just,' he begins a new thought, stumbling over his words a little. 'Sorry, I realise that you wouldn't want to be getting in a car with a strange man, I…'

He seems embarrassed for having offered now.

'Though my friends would tell you I'm only a bit strange.'

He flashes the wide smile again, using humour to deflect the social awkwardness.

'It's okay,' Zoya says firmly. 'I'm going to wait for my friend.'

There is no friend. She wonders if the man can tell.

'Ah, okay then,' he responds, shaking his head at his own stupidity and releasing the handbrake.

Zoya steps back a few paces.

'Are you sure, then? You don't want a lift?'

Zoya nods.

'I just, don't think I've seen anyone else on the roads. Do you want me to just wait here until your friend comes?'

'Ah, no, I'll wait for my friend. Keeps me warm; walking.'

'Sure, okay then. Sorry I bothered you… I just feel bad now, leaving you on your own in the cold, dark night. Okay then, final offer' – he drops the handbrake – 'you don't need a lift?'

'No, I'm fine. Thanks. Goodbye.'

He looks at her and revs the engine unexpectedly loudly, before speeding off into the night.

As he drove off, it seemed like he was saying something she didn't quite catch, masked by the engine sound. The car has disappeared now, burrowing into the dark, leafy lane, but her mind keeps turning over the sound of it, like an echo. Maybe she is just paranoid, but didn't he say her name?

'Bye, Zoya'?

She stands there quietly, starting to feel cold and half expecting to hear his car coming back again. It doesn't. Or at least, not *yet*.

She sets off walking with purpose again. Glad to be powered by her own choices and her own two feet.

She gets into a rhythm: left, right, left, right, left, right... *Bye, Zoya. Bye, Zoya. Bye, Zoya...*

CHAPTER 25

Zoya walks on, into the night. The car doesn't come back. Not yet.

Because she had been dancing and then rushing Olivia to the hospital, she isn't wearing a watch. Time seems to be looping around her, dark and slippy, like an oil leak. She wonders how late it is getting.

She walks on at pace, recognising clumps of bushes and familiar curves of the road. At first, they seem to mark her progress but then seem to be recurring on a loop. *It's all fine*, she tells herself. *There's just one, simple route back and it's not so far and I can walk around four miles an hour.*

She is getting used to the night now – the dark tunnels of trees and the moonlit reprieves. The way ahead seems particularly shadowy, but all she needs to see is the road beneath her feet. She is saving her torch battery for when she really needs it, finding her way just fine in the dark.

Then she stands stock still. There is a lumpen dead thing on the road.

'Shit,' she whispers, edging closer, looking at the carcass and hating herself. This is the 'fox' she thought she ran over on the way here – except it isn't a fox, it's a dog.

She doesn't know why that would make a difference, but it does. She shines her torch on the animal: open eyes, glassy and lifeless; a twisted pose, dead-weight limbs. She doesn't see a collar. Blood has matted some of the fur and stains the white bib beneath the dog's lifeless, dislocated jaw.

She can see the texture of the greying tongue, panting no more. The torch blinks out as the battery dies and Zoya doesn't care. The darkness seems more respectful, somehow. What are you meant to do with dead strays?

Whatever it is, she's not really in a position to deal with it right now. She drops the torch and sets off walking again, following the white markings of the road. Black shadows follow her.

Branches swipe at her face, looming out of the darkness, almost quick enough to scratch an eye. She can hear her footsteps echoing in the lane. She isn't yet paranoid enough to think that they are the steps of someone behind her – but the idea briefly flashes through her mind.

But this time, she can't turn her thoughts off, can't focus quite so single-mindedly on the one-step-after-another of the long walk home. She casts her mind back to that conversation with Sharon, where she talked of her hopes of reunion with the ex. She hadn't encouraged Sharon to see him, had she? Hadn't supported the idea of inviting him to the theatre, hadn't suggested she tell him where she is?

Was.

Zoya had never, for a minute, considered that Sharon might have been involved with someone abusive, because she, herself, never had. Sharon's death would forever be a reminder that there are all sorts of people in the world, living all sorts of lives, and dealing with all sorts of problems that she knows nothing about. Zoya, with all her privileges, knows nothing, she realises. Nothing at all.

No, she knows one thing: innocent people die.

One woman, murdered by her own father, her body hidden in a garden shed. One man, so desperate to be someone else, dying on a bloody pavement, gathering a crowd. One man, loved and lauded, not able to survive his blackest cloud. One woman shrinking herself out of existence and to an early grave. And Sharon, so hopeful and loving, killed, no doubt, by the anger of a man.

So what if someone assumes Zoya likes 'world music', or calls her 'Miss' instead of 'Ms', or gets her to change a dance routine?

Zoya hears a strange sound in the darkness and then identifies it as coming from her own mouth. She is, for a moment, overtaken by sobbing and it comes out like a ghostly gasp.

She shakes her head and dries her cheeks with her hands, looking back into the blackness before striding on.

She can hear the rush of night winds over the open fields. It sounds like the slow roll of tyres tailing her path.

If that man is the one who killed Sharon and he is driving around here at night and he somehow knows who Zoya is – what does he want? Where is he going? What is he looking for? How does he know her name? Did Sharon talk about her? Does he know that she has been asking about *him*? That she got his car reported to the police? She thinks, with a shiver, of what might have happened if she *had* got into that car.

Suddenly, she thinks of the dance school, all transparent and fragile and unsuspecting in the night. She thinks of the gates, always open, and the small wooden sign pointing out just where they are.

She has to get back there – *there*, where she has been going all night – if she can just get back and get the gates closed, she would feel better about everything, and about everyone inside. She thinks of everyone sleeping in their beds.

She remembers all that money that Sharon was trying to keep under her bed. That must be what he is after. That must be what he wanted the night he killed her – and he still wants it now.

She starts to jog, though it seems an effort, lifting her heavy legs and slapping her feet, one after another, along the road. Her breath sounds loud in the darkness now, underscored by the trickle of tiny stones being dislodged by her soles, almost masking the sound of creeping wheels.

She slows when she sees her own shadow cast before her, growing taller, more distorted by the spread of headlights approaching from behind. Her feet stumble to a stop. He *has* been following her all along. She freezes. Ice shoots along her spine.

A car door opens and she jerks around to look. She can't see anything but the headlights – and a figure advancing in the dark.

CHAPTER 26

The man approaches slowly. Zoya feels herself backing away. She squints to look through the glaring headlights, peering at the movement in the shadows beyond.

She wishes she had torchlight to shine at him and at least *know*. She wishes she had the dead torch even – something to swing or throw.

He is walking in front of the vehicle now, his shoulders a sharp silhouette. Zoya's eyes water with the glare of it. Her feet jittery, ready to run.

'What are the chances?'

A man's voice emerges from the dark.

Zoya straightens up. She recognises that frame, those shoulders.

'What!?' she snaps incredulously.

Her fists un-ball and fly into a wild, open-palmed gesture.

'It... it's me, Reed. I thought you'd laugh, I... We always say that... Hey, is everything okay?'

Zoya steps out of the glare now and sees the familiar Volkswagen camper purring reliably in the lane.

'No. Yes! I'm fine but... were you trying to scare me?'

'Of course not. Are you really okay? Why are you out here alone? Why are you running?'

Zoya focusses on the task in hand again.

'We've got to get back to the school.'

Reed's head bobs in the outline of the light, nodding amiably.

'Come *on*,' Zoya instructs, making for the open door.

'What, no hug hello then?'

Zoya pauses to look at him.

'*Now*, Reed. Now!'

'Hey, hey, shush' – Reed puts a finger to his lips – 'Dan's in there, sleeping.'

Zoya rolls her eyes and clambers into the driving seat.

'No, no,' Reed says, standing on the road beside her. '*I'll* drive.'

Zoya sighs and clambers across to the passenger seat as he gets in.

She peers around to look at the tangle of duvet behind them in the shadowy cabin.

'Aw,' she says quietly, looking at Reed with shining eyes. 'Like a baby!'

She watches Reed fastening his seatbelt, suddenly full of fond gratitude to see him again. He catches her expression: wry and pensive.

'So, where do *you* sleep then?' she asks.

He shrugs a little in response.

'We sometimes buddy up,' he says.

She grins at him and they laugh together.

'So,' he asks, 'what was the rush?'

'Just get us back to the dance school as quick as we can, and I'll tell you the rest there.'

'Okay, but I'm not sure I can find it in the dark... It's quite hidden, isn't it?'

'I *hope* so,' Zoya replies, causing him to frown at her. 'Doesn't matter,' she says. 'Just drive.'

***

At the mouth of the driveway, Zoya is tugging and pulling at the metal gate. Heavy leaves flap with every yank as the spring foliage seems reluctant to let it go. She keeps pulling, but the cold bars, like obstinate deathly fingers, scratch sharp rust against her skin and do not move. The overgrown bushes shake in protest, fighting with woody claws to keep their grip.

Reed hops out of the van, which he has now tucked beside the bushes, clear of the gateway, killing the engine and – on her instruction – the lights.

'Wouldn't it be better if you could see what you were doing?' he asks rationally, still bemused about what is going on.

'No, shhh, this is fine.'

She pulls again at the old gate. She stops and looks at Reed who is hovering by the van.

'*Help* me, then,' she says.

He takes hold of the bars. Together they tear the gate out of the bushes. It comes free, juddering as it swings. They reunite it with the post.

They look at one another with moonlit faces, hers determined, his somewhat scared. Zoya turns a bolt into its long-lost hole and the iron makes a small groan. Then Reed sees her eyes light up to discover an old padlock hung on the gate.

'Don't!' he whispers urgently, but she locks it triumphantly and steps back.

He watches as she begins wading across the shadowy night grasses.

'That might never come open again, you know…' he says, following her, his knees bobbing high above the long grass.

'Aren't you forgetting something?' she asks, turning toward him.

He stands, befuddled and blank-faced.

'We can open any doors…?' she says, reminding him. 'We can sort it out when we're asleep.'

'Oh… yeah… I never thought about…'

He follows her again.

'But anyway, Zoya, wait.' His voice builds to a stage whisper. '*Wait!*'

She stops walking and looks at him.

'What's going on?'

***

They are sitting in the camper again, talking with soft, low voices, their watchful eyes sweeping the scene. The old block stands silently, like an ice cube above the shifting stretch of grass.

'So, if it *is* him…'

'… prowling the lanes,' Zoya says, filling in.

'… what do you think he wants?'

Zoya's knee is bouncing, slight but fast.

'One of two things, I think.'

'What?'

'Well, I saw her with all this money, you see, a big bag of cash… but where's that now?'

She turns her gaze back to survey the sleepy grounds.

The shuffling trees that line the driveway drift off behind the extension to crouch angularly, in black, conspiratorial clumps. On the other side, the shifting swathe of silvery grasses presents a brighter picture, but the endlessly flowing leaves seem to whisper behind her back.

'And the second option?'

'It's just that someone told me…'

'What?'

'That he'd been asking about me… by name.'

'Zoya!'

'*Shhh!*' she hisses, glancing behind them to the cabin.

Reed lowers his voice and quells his agitation.

'I see – you've been going around saying things and talking to people, haven't you? Zoya – we don't even need to do that! What's wrong with a simple bit of sleep-sleuthing? Nobody even needs to know. Hey, why are we trying not to wake Dan, anyway? He's a big guy, might be good to have around in a fight.'

'Shhh,' Zoya repeats, shaking her head.

'I don't think he's going to get through that rusty gate. Don't you think maybe you overreac–'

Zoya looks at him murderously, cutting off the word he was about to say. Then she turns away to scour the shadowy perimeter. He can see her shaking her head.

'I don't think you should have locked that gate, though...'

She glances at him, sideways, listening for what he's going to say.

'What if we need the police out here? Or an ambulance?'

Zoya's expression rumples with annoyance and regret but she doesn't say anything aloud.

'Why don't we just go in? I'll walk you to the door – stay with you inside, whatever, whatever you want.'

He lays a hand on her arm to get her to look at him. She holds his gaze for a moment then looks back at the bed again.

'What about Dan?'

'Let him sleep,' Reed says. 'There's nothing going on.'

The scene *does* seem peacefully quiet, a pleasant breeze rolling its way along the lawn.

'Do you know what it is?' Zoya asks, her voice relaxing as she smiles.

Reed shakes his head and raises his eyebrows.

'I think I'm just used to it being me and you... in the night... exploring.'

He contemplates her face, then nods, understanding what she means.

'So, are we going in?' he asks, eventually.

'That's the other thing.' She shoots him an awkward look. 'I lost my keys.'

Reed studies the assortment of buildings and extensions ahead of them.

'So there must be some back door somewhere, left unopened?'

'I hope not!'

'Shit, yeah, I mean, no, I'm sure it's all locked up – like it always is…'

'No, it's okay' – her palm on his thigh for a moment – 'it will be. There's a whole thing. It's all properly locked up every night.'

'Or we could just stay here,' Reed suggests. 'Maybe even…?'

He turns his head to look at the sleeping mound in the back.

'Really?' Zoya's eyebrow rises. 'All three of us squeezed in the back there?'

'Why not? We're all buddies here. Anyway, you can have the roof bed – any time you want…'

Zoya leans her head back on the headrest, chuckling, until a strobe of light splashes through the bushes from the road. Her face falls, but the vehicle doesn't slow or stop.

'It's okay. It wasn't him,' she says, but her words come out wavering on her breath. 'And he can't get in now, any-way,' she continues.

'Unless – he's already inside?'

'No. It's unlikely,' she says determinedly. 'I've got an idea though.' She peers and points at a certain part of the building. 'See that low block there?'

'No. Where? What are you going to do?'

'You know how I like to jump off places?'

Reed's expression becomes crooked with confusion.

'Well,' Zoya goes on, 'what comes down, must first go up…'

CHAPTER 27

Reed wobbles a bit, clutching Zoya's ankles, her feet on his shoulders.

'I really think this is a job for Dan…' he whispers, staring at the wall in front of his face.

'No, I'm nearly there now, just let go of my right foot… My *other* right!!'

He hears her scrabbling at the guttering overhead, her weight evaporating as she climbs.

'Okay, I'm up.'

Reed steps back uncertainly, holding out his arms in case she slips. He sees her up on top of the corridor roof, already disappearing away from the edge.

He looks uneasily from side to side. They are closer to the dark woods back here. *There could easily be someone hiding in those deep shadows*, he thinks – but doesn't say a thing.

Zoya's face appears at the edge of the roof again, whispering instructions.

'This is good – I'll be able to get up onto the main bit from here. It's fine – I know what the rooftop is like up there; I go there all the time. There's a door that leads back inside – never locked. I'll just go in and then open up that door for you. You go back there.' She points at the residential block at the rear of the main building. 'Just go around and wait for me there.'

He looks up at her. Her eyes seem serious and dark. Reed nods.

'Are you going to be alright getting up there?'

'Yes. It'll be fine. And how are you going to help me from down there anyway? Go on – I won't be long.'

She watches as he paces backwards. He looks concerned.

'Don't worry. I'm a good climber, remember?'

He knows that she is.

Then Zoya disappears away from the edge to start her climb, so Reed sets off obediently, his feet wading through the uncut grass, making a soft, swishing path as he goes.

Zoya begins her climb. The wood panelling and drainpipe afford her easy holds and the adrenaline coursing through her veins keeps her strong and focussed and fast.

She reaches the high wall and sees the roof space – hoping that the access door hasn't been randomly locked. She swings her legs over the wall and drops gently to the surface. It only takes a minute to catch her breath.

She sees the small wooden door – slightly ajar, as usual. She feels a sense of relief. It pays to explore places, she thinks.

Something makes her pace to the other side of the building and take a look over the site. The grounds look just as peaceful over there. The outbuildings by the distant perimeter are cast in blocky black shadow by the bright, clear moon, and the sweep of shining grasses stills her. She looks at the old, outdoor stage, wondering why it just stands there, dilapidated and unused.

Then she gets the sense of movement in her peripheral vision – a small shadow darting below the far trees. Beneath the fluttering leaves and shadowy branches, something is racing in a straight line.

She narrows her eyes.

A small car emerges from the shadowy treeline and tears across the lawn. She can hear its engine now; growling as it cuts a wild, muddy slash across the ground.

Zoya watches open-mouthed, flinching when the vehicle cracks the edge of the outdoor stage, smashing a set of wooden steps. She has to assume it is *him* again – Sharon's killer.

He is heading for the main hall now, set on a determined course. He'll have to start slowing soon, she thinks, but the car races, faster and faster, toward the wall of glass.

She holds her breath.

The crash shocks her skeleton. She can feel the impact vibrating through her feet. That's the sound of glass smashing, of the world tumbling down.

Her feet do the thinking next, carrying her toward the door that leads inside. She yanks it open and hurries down the small stairway that seems to tilt and twist. It's dark but her feet know the way.

She didn't see the impact beneath her, but she has to get down – down to the earth now, in case the building starts to give way.

She emerges on the first-floor landing, the sound of blood pulsing through her ears. The tipping and swaying motion, she soon realises, is only coming from inside her head. She stands gawping at the destruction – the battered car slumped through the window, the staircase crumpling around the wreck. The glass that once stood smooth and perfect is everywhere, like ice, and a chasm of night air is spilling inside.

Then her ears clear and all the sounds come crashing in. A man's voice is ripping through the shattered space.

She can see him now, lumbering around the car. It's the same car that she saw in the lanes. He is dragging something heavy with him and shouting. He looks up and notices her standing on the mezzanine. She sees the moonlight shining wetly on his bloodied scalp. It is also glinting menacingly from the object hanging at his side.

The staircase has caught some of the impact, splintering and dropping on one side, but it's still mostly *there*. He is making his way up the stairs now, moving toward her, and the thing he is dragging is an axe.

'Look what you made me do!' he roars.

Zoya's mouth feels dry.

'I want my money!'

He throws a twisted leg up onto the next step, grasping the one railing that remains intact.

'You fucking bitches!' he wails.

The axe grinds horribly against the stairs.

'Look what you made me do! My Capri! My money! Sharon… *She* took them! Fucking bitches – you're all the same.'

Zoya turns on the balls of her feet and dashes away – back to the staircase that leads up to the roof. It doesn't make much sense, but her instinct is to climb.

Out on the roof again, she runs one way, then another, the grounds outside a swimming sea of shadow and light. There is no way out. It feels so wrong to her – to be so high and feel so trapped.

Now, there is noise and light and voices. People are spilling out into the night, barefoot and shouting and confused.

The wooden door bangs behind her – perhaps ricocheting from her exit or perhaps flung open by *him*. Instinctively, she makes for the wall – she's got to get back down.

A shout sounds from below. Leon is standing out in front of the building, desperately calling her name.

She gets on top of the wall closest to him. He is in vest and jogging bottoms down there, barefoot and bare-armed, standing steady and strong.

'The building's not safe, Zoya! You have to get down.'

He bends his arms toward her and nods his head. She can see the curves of his muscles and thinks of all the experience and skill and practice he has used to sculpt all that strength.

'It's not that high, Zoya. Come on, I'll catch you. Remember – the swing dissipates the momentum. I'll swing you around my body and then you can roll out of it. It's really, really soft grass.'

She looks at him, inhaling courage and air. It feels cool, deep inside her lungs.

'Come on, we've done this before.'

Zoya nods. Leon nods. Zoya nods again.

Then she pushes herself away from the wall, dropping with precision toward him.

Falling.

And then they are rolling on the thick grass. No bones feel broken.

They lie there, panting, not quite believing it – any of it. The moon is full and cratered and bright.

'I can see you!' comes the claggy, gravelly voice. It sounds perversely sing-song amid the shuffling and the scattering of glass splinters and the metallic slide of the dragging axe.

They look up to see the man coming for them. He is framed by the cave of shattered glass, still shouting and moving and crazed. He lurches slowly in the atrium toward the hole torn open by the crash.

Their mouths drop open. Then something falls on top of him and flattens him to the ground. They scramble to their feet. It wasn't debris but a person who lies there and moans: Toby.

Toby has thrown himself on top of their attacker from the balcony above. He is wincing but basically fine. They rush inside and right him and pull him away from the man.

Alex is now silent and still on the floor, perhaps uncon-scious, his grip finally loosed from the axe.

Toby's leg seems painful, so they take his weight around their shoulders and support him as he limps. As they help Toby outside, Zoya looks back to see that the door to the first-floor office is bright with light.

'What are you even doing here?' Zoya insists incredulously.

'Tax returns,' Toby replies, sounding perfectly matter-of-fact.

'I told you, Zoya,' Leon says, 'Toby's the best human you will ever meet.'

They limp through the gaping hole where the window used to be and into the fresh breezes and the dawning light.

CHAPTER 28

By dawn, everything looks different.

People are scattered, talking in groups, wandering arm in arm or sitting on the grass. To Zoya, it feels like the aftermath of a music festival or the slow, second wave of a party where people have stayed up to watch the sunrise.

The lawns are sprinkled with delicate grass flowers and bright daisies revealing themselves to the sun. Songbirds are chirping quietly in the greenery, gathering energy for the day of flitting and flirting ahead.

Someone got the padlock open to let the authorities in, and Sharon's ex has already been removed in a police ambulance. Firemen are inspecting the structural damage to the building and Toby is being checked over by paramedics near the gate.

Zoya and Leon sit, wearing foil blankets, in the middle of the grassy expanse.

'There he goes, the local hero,' Leon says, as they watch Toby being helped into the ambulance.

He waves at them calmly, seeming just as self-deprecating as earlier, when he deflected all their repeated thanks and praise. Zoya waves back at him gently.

'I'm surprised he's even letting them take him for X-rays,' she says.

He gets in and they watch the ambulance driving off into the lane.

Sandy, Tilda and Lauren walk up to them, wearing their nightclothes.

'Are you sure you're okay, you two?' Tilda asks.

Zoya looks down at her limbs, all miraculously intact.

'Yeah. Yeah, we're okay,' she responds.

'So, what…' Lauren begins.

'… happened?' Leon says, finishing her sentence.

He looks at Zoya.

'Don't look at *me*,' she says. 'I've never seen that man before in my life.'

Not before the car in the lanes, she thinks, remembering, with a shudder, how close she was to getting in.

'But he's the one who murdered Sharon, though,' Sandy says seriously.

Zoya looks at the hole in the front of the building and remembers his angry shouting.

'Fairly certain,' she says, staring at the mess.

Everyone trades sad almost-smiles and Leon puts an arm around Zoya.

'It's that *guy*,' Tilda says and Zoya turns to see Reed approaching, his lanky legs stepping through the sweep of long grass.

'Who is it?' Leon asks.

'Dunno,' Sandy says, 'but he was really good in a crisis.'

They greet him with friendly smiles as he ambles into earshot. Zoya has cocked her head and raised an eyebrow, curious to find out what they mean.

'Yeah,' Lauren adds, 'he was at the back door directing everyone to go behind the trees.'

Reed can hear them talking about him and looks bashful.

'They're saying you can go back inside the residential block now, if you like,' he offers.

'Yeah, let's go and get showered,' Tilda says, and they set off walking.

Sandy plants his hand on Reed's shoulder.

'Thanks, man,' he says, then walks off with the other friends.

'And there I was, thinking you were hiding in the woods,' Zoya teases, shaking her head slightly.

Reed shrugs performatively.

'Hey, what can I say? Some of us are natural born leaders… level-headed… intelligent… trustworthy…'

Zoya laughs her gentle laugh.

'We can't all be,' Reed pauses, shocked at the up-close sight of Leon's strikingly muscled shoulders but committed to finishing his thought, '… action heroes. Some of us are just strong in other…'

He breaks away from the sentence to lean down and clasp Leon's hands in an enthusiastic handshake, no longer able to keep up his wry facade.

'Man, you were fucking awesome, wow! How did you not break your arms catching her like that? That was fucking insane!'

Leon laughs and lets his hand be vigorously shaken.

'Leon, this is Reed,' Zoya says, introducing them.

'So, what brings *you* here?' Leon asks by way of greeting.

It seems an oddly formal question, amid all the devastation, so the three of them share an infectious chuckle.

'And don't say your van!' Zoya quips, predicting his reply.

They laugh with relief. Zoya feels lightness washing over her.

Leon follows their gaze to see the Neptune Blue camper van shining in the morning light.

'Nice motor,' he says just as the door is opening.

Out clambers a man in shorts and dressing gown, his bird's nest of curls sticking up on his head. One eye seems sticky with sleep and he is wiggling a finger in an ear.

He walks, stumbling slightly over the thick waves of grass, toward the friends he recognises, turning slowly to take in the strange scene. There are small clumps of people hanging around, also wearing nightclothes, which evidently confuses him, and he clearly doesn't even know where he is.

He approaches the group – like a toddler unsure of his steps – and takes in the building and the fire brigade tape, double-taking when he sees the crashed car about to be hauled away. Zoya and Leon join Reed on their feet.

'And who's *this* sleepy bear?' Leon asks as they all watch.

Dan nears the group and looks slowly from one friend to the other to the stranger and then starts the sequence all over again. His face so clearly conveys his question – *what did I miss?* – that he never needs to say the words.

Zoya smiles.

'And this is Dan.'

CHAPTER 29

'We've been here before,' Zoya says, not looking me in the eye.

I look around at the stage, noticing the wooden steps that were smashed by the car.

We are sitting on the old outdoor stage in the grounds of the school. It is set in a sunken circle with raked steps for the audience that rise to meet the gentle hill. The neglected arcs of paving diminish in the grass like the ripples of a pebble in a pond. The foot of the stage is also messy with loose grit and wayward twigs. The structure smells of rotten wood and moss and rust.

I look up at the rigging. Above us, posts and beams cut angles through a roofless sky. There are stars twinkling in the darkness.

'*I* haven't,' I reply, looking at her again.

Then I remember the Titania Theatre stage, back in Shilly-on-Sea, and wonder if that's what she means.

A faint breeze flutters the fine curl hanging by her cheek. She is staring ahead and looks sad.

'No, we've been here before' – she looks at me gravely – 'talking about the way someone died.'

I lower my head and let my gaze rest on my knees, my legs dangling over the edge of the stage.

'Ah.' I swing one leg slightly so that the heel of my Converse butts the wood a few times. 'Yeah,' I agree darkly.

Zoya makes a spluttering noise, almost resembling laughter, and her face takes on the grotesque mimicry of glee.

'And the thing is – it was exactly what I thought it was all along! The violent ex-boyfriend.' She laughs grimly. 'Like a fucking pantomime!'

She kicks the stage with the back of her boot now; once, hard. I stop my swinging. For some reason, images of a Punch and Judy show flash horribly through my mind.

We sit quietly, side by side, thinking about Alex Belasis' confession. The night winds ruffle the thick perimeter of summer trees beyond the long lawns; leaves rustling over leaves like whispers. I watch the moonlight playing on the lifting boughs.

I remember sitting on that pale beach with her a lifetime ago, trying to say the right thing about Donna – and failing. I remember the smell of her skin as we talked in a soft Edinburgh bed about what I knew and *didn't* know about Marcus and whether I should keep it to myself.

I still don't know why Sharon would have got in the car with Alex that night when she already knew he wasn't there to make amends, wasn't interested in seeing her in the show, wasn't suddenly, miraculously, 'a great guy'.

I think about that orange Capri. I've sat in that passenger seat. I got in without giving it a moment's thought. I don't say anything.

'I've been on that hillside,' Zoya says soberly, 'where the rocks are.'

We seem to be having parallel thoughts.

We look at one another. She doesn't say any more, but I know where and what she means – the hillside where Sharon tasted the cool, high air and felt the breath of the earth for the last time; the rocky outcrop where a man's rage took her life.

At least she wasn't alive when he dropped her over the bridge, I thought, when they told us – but there's no 'at least' about it, just my own selfish fear giving itself away. I just wanted to be rid of that image; of someone falling – screaming – to their death.

Zoya looks like she is picturing something herself.

She also has that guilty look she has been carrying around with her recently, matched by stooped shoulders and bowed head.

'You know… that taxi driver,' I begin. 'He wouldn't have told them what he'd seen if you hadn't persuaded him to, and maybe, without that, Alex Belasis would never have confessed.'

Zoya goes back to looking at the concrete. She sighs nasally and concedes the tiniest smile possible at the very edge of her mouth. As a way to cheer her up, what I've pointed out is grim and hopeless – but it's also true.

She looks at me out of the corner of her eye.

'You haven't said it yet.'

'What?' I ask, confused.

'But you're thinking it,' she continues. 'Don't worry, we all are: *why did she even get in his car?*'

I nod, then swallow.

'Why did she invite him down here, do you think?' I ask. 'After doing such a good job of getting away?'

'I don't know,' Zoya says, the words spilling out on sighing breath. 'Because it wasn't actually a pantomime – because Alex wasn't some moustache twirler come to get her – he was actually someone she knew and loved. There must have been good times...'

'But she'd already decided to leave him.'

Zoya nods her head gently.

'Yeah. What I've read about these things – it's complicated.' She sighs, sharply this time. 'You know what I think?'

I look at her warily.

'I think it's because of hope.'

I feel a strange shiver run down my spine, even though it is as warm as ever in the dreaming tonight.

'And I always thought that hope was a good thing,' I say.

She looks pensive.

'I suppose it depends which side of the river you are looking from.'

She looks into the distance.

'Did you know that one in four women experience domestic abuse at some point in their lives? One in four! I read that too.'

I think about Zoya and Sharon and Tilda and Lauren… about Jane and Issy and Cally and Karen… about the Popplewell sisters and Catriona Reece… about Aunt Abigail and Sarah Stevens and Rhoda Sorrel and Donna Verity.

One in four.

Zoya lies down so that her back is resting on the stage. She is looking up at the constellations.

'You can change the subject now,' she says. 'I mean, I *want* you to. *Please* do.'

She is lying on the boards, her hair spilling around her like a dark halo. I wonder what she is inviting me to do.

Then I lie down, rolling my spine to rest on the floor beside her. The old metal rigging frames the stars above.

'Didn't you say you were having thoughts about this place?' I ask her.

'Yeah.' She leans on her elbows, surveying the structure thoughtfully. 'I just don't know why they don't use this anymore; wouldn't take that much work to get it up to scratch.'

'Yeah,' I agree. I think the whole dance group could probably use a project right now. 'Why don't you suggest it?'

I watch her as she considers her plan and I notice her shoulders relax. I'm not sure who they could get for an audience, though, all the way out here, hidden behind the trees.

***

The next morning, the dance group are holding their daily digest – in some ways just as usual, in others, really, *really* not.

Instead of the atrium and canteen tables, they are sitting on the thick, grassy lawn. Jerrod and Meredith are standing before the group and a discussion is underway.

Beyond them, Zoya can see the boarded-up windows on the main building. Then she stretches her neck, raising her face to the morning sun. The tranquillity of the bright scene doesn't match the seriousness of the matter in hand.

'We don't want to set down any rules here,' Jerrod is saying. 'Genuinely, we need to consider, as a group, whether to go ahead with the Midsummer Show or not.'

His sombre gaze rolls around the group, focussing on individuals, one by one.

Zoya finds herself looking around the group too; lots of the dancers are looking from friend to friend.

A short distance away by the trees is Reed's van. Reed and Dan have also been furnished with breakfast and coffee and are busying themselves with chatting, squinting and making sure not to look like they are listening in.

Reed is sitting in the open cabin door with his toes buried in the grass, sipping coffee and thumbing through a newspaper. Dan is standing next to him, engaging in a series of morning stretches, his T-shirt riding up over his belly as he moves.

Zoya notices Leon watching him and is surprised by the shine in his eyes. He turns back to listen to the directors.

'So,' Meredith is saying, 'we're not saying this has to be the final decision, but it would be helpful, as a starting point, if we could get a feel for what you are all thinking…'

'Raise your hand if you want to go ahead with the performance,' Jerrod says, again sweeping the circle with his gaze.

Everybody raises their hands.

For Sharon's sake, Zoya thinks.

'Okay, thanks everyone,' Meredith says. 'Thanks for expressing that. We wanted to get your thoughts on that one first… because' – her voice slows – 'because we didn't want that decision to be influenced by some news we've had.'

Backs straighten and expressions stiffen around the group.

'It's just that the theatre have been in touch. They're going to have to close down' – Jerrod damps down the rising concern of the group with flattening hand gestures – 'not forever, just while they sort out a faulty wiring problem. I know, I know, it really leaves us in the lurch but it's for fire safety so…'

What is it with old theatres and fires? Zoya wonders but takes it as a cue to raise her idea.

'I know,' she calls out confidently. 'We can just use the outdoor stage. I've been taking a look; wouldn't take that much effort – or money – to make it nice again. Less than hiring a theatre, I would guess…?'

'Yeah, let's do it!' Ivan yells.

'Yeah, it's perfect,' Jo adds.

There seems to be a positive reception to the idea.

'We'll help.'

Zoya looks up to see that Dan and Reed have wandered over to join in.

Meredith smiles broadly at Zoya.

'That's another great idea you've had!'

'Oh?' Jerrod says. 'What's the other?'

Most of the group start chatting about the stage project now but Zoya pays close attention to the directors' conversation unfolding at the front.

Meredith turns to Jerrod.

'We're opening up a community programme for young people in the area,' she states pleasantly.

Jerrod frowns.

'No, we've been through this,' he says. 'We're not a community organisation. We're... our *own* community. Come on, Meredith, we've discussed this before. We can't maintain our focus on the artistic development if we open ourselves up to all and sundry... It's not...'

He is shaking his head.

'Jerrod. You seem to be forgetting that while you are director of the programme, *I* am the director of the New Movement School. It's *my* call and that's what we're doing.' She smiles again in Zoya's direction, nodding toward her in gesture. 'And we already have a volunteer substitute driver.'

Jerrod looks down at her, long enough for Zoya to display a humble, hopeful little smile. Then he sighs and walks off back to the buildings.

Meredith raises her voice to address the group again and everyone pays attention.

'One other thing: I'd like each performing group to stop by my office at some point today – not all at once – with the titles for your pieces for the programme.' She pauses. 'Have a think. Okay, that's it for now, then. The studios will be open, schedules on the doors…'

The dancers collect up the breakfast debris and spring to their feet, gathering in groups and strolling back toward the school.

Zoya smiles at Reed and Dan, who already seem to be planning the renovations, pointing and gesticulating at different parts of the stage. She will catch up with them later. For now, there are others she needs to speak to.

She hops lightly over the springy turf, looking for Clare, Jo or Gemma. She finds them clustered together, already discussing performance titles as they walk.

'Hey.' Zoya catches them and puts a hand on Clare's shoulder. 'Hey.' The others notice her too. 'I've got a title for you – for your piece, if you want it?'

They stand looking at her, waiting to hear the suggestion.

Zoya swallows to lubricate her throat.

'*The Never-Ending Fall,*' she suggests.

Gemma cocks her head, sympathetically.

'But that's *your* title,' she says.

'No, no, it's much better for your piece than mine; I want you to use it.'

'Thanks,' Jo says. She seems to understand the significance.

'Besides,' Zoya says, 'now that I've put lifts in my piece with Leon, it doesn't suit my choreography. I'm thinking my title should be something more to do with… flight.'

MAY

CHAPTER 30

Zoya enters the café and looks around. Someone is tackling one of the giant scones. Seeing only a handful of customers and no staff, she approaches the counter and begins rummaging in her bag for a stack of flyers.

'Hello again.'

She looks up to see Brian emerging from the kitchen with a checked tea towel over one shoulder.

'Hi. Would it be okay if I leave some flyers here? It's for the dance school show. Saturday the twentieth of June. We're doing it up at the school this time. Everyone welcome.'

Brian picks up the topmost flyer and starts reading.

'Are you from the dance school?' a voice asks.

Zoya looks up and locates the speaker. A burly man in paint-splattered overalls is looking at her.

'Yes?' Zoya answers uncertainly.

'My son has been going to your classes – I've never seen him so buzzed.'

Zoya smiles and hand-delivers a flyer to the man at his table, placing it by his plate of chips.

'Then you've got to come see the performance.' She points at the details on the flyer. 'It's free.'

The father nods and starts tucking the flyer away in his pocket.

'I never even knew it was there, before,' he says.

'There's a map on the flyer,' Zoya says, walking casually backwards. 'Bring people!'

Zoya gathers her bag full of flyers.

'Hey.' Brian catches her attention just before she leaves. 'I just wanted to say that... I'm glad that...' – he looks her in the eye, probably thinking about Sharon – 'I'm glad that you're doing this.'

Zoya conveys her understanding with a smile, leaves the shop and walks down the stone steps.

*****

A little later, she stops to check her watch. She probably has enough time to flyer the pub before getting back to the dance school to give the volunteers their lifts home.

Turning a corner, she almost bumps into someone. They have been here before.

Jozek Malish stands before her, watching her reaction, too many layers of emotion shining in his eyes. Their pause stretches on a little longer than it might have. It feels important that they have run into one another, but neither one can come up with anything to say.

Zoya thinks for a moment, deciding to choose positivity. She slips her hand into her bag and holds a flyer out for him. Her hand and her spirits drop slowly as she watches his gaze fall to his shuffling feet.

'It's for a free dance show up at the school...' Zoya explains in a voice that trails away.

He looks sideways and avoids her steady gaze.

'We're moving to Luton. My brother has an electrical business there – the boys can work shifts after school.'

'You're leaving…?' Zoya responds.

She notices the direction of Jozek's gaze, his eyes focussed on a spot in the distant landscape. She can't help turning around to look.

It's nothing really – just a tuck in the greying hills beyond the town. You wouldn't even know the ravine bridge was there, unless you knew it – and you might not know what happened to Sharon there, even if you did.

'It will be good for them,' Jozek says, flicking his eyes back to Zoya's for a rare instance of eye contact.

Then his voice strains against a cracking whisper.

'I can't stay here anymore.'

Zoya slips the flyer back into her bag. They stand there at the corner for a while, almost nodding.

'Miss… er…?'

'Zoya,' she says, offering her first name.

'I really hope everything goes well.'

He smiles a weak smile and they pass one another, continuing on in their separate journeys.

***

Inside the pub, Zoya lingers at the end of the bar, hoping to grab someone's attention.

She sees the same bright windows, thick with curtains, lighting the smoky fug and illuminating pink cheeks and sparkling eyes. She hears the same hubbub of football chat, wild opinion and wheezing laughter, swelling and sinking in a comforting rhythm. She recognises the same locals in the same clothes eating the same meals.

When Zach appears, she can't help grinning.

'Zoya! Hi,' he says, coming closer.

'Hi, Zach. How's it going?'

He smiles and shrugs.

'Can't complain.'

Zoya looks along the bar but can't see any place for flyers. Wet rings from pint glasses pattern the worn wooden surface.

'I heard about what happened… You're the hero of the hour, aren't you?'

Zoya feels her cheeks flush.

'Oh no, I… I didn't do anything… I was just *there*…'

She rummages in the bag for a handful of flyers, keen to change the subject.

'And it was the arsehole who killed your friend? How did they get him? You know, nobody had even mentioned him until you…'

'Well, he confessed, so… Anyway, I was just wondering if… I mean I don't think you have flyers here, do you, but…'

'Oh, I don't know… I'll ask.'

'The reason you don't see any other flyers,' Lynn says, coming over, drying her hand on a cloth, and taking the wad from Zoya, 'is that nobody else round here does anything worth advertising.' She reads the contents for a second. 'Of course we'll have them, love.'

She smiles and finds a couple of prominent spots to set them out around the pub.

For a second, being called 'love' in a northern accent like that, reminds Zoya of her dad, and it feels like she hasn't seen him for a very long time. He still doesn't know anything about any of it, because she didn't want to ruin his plans. They will be away again now, in Chicago, she realises, working out their itinerary in her mind.

And, before she can wish that Richard and Abigail could be there at the end-of-year performance, after all, she realises that it is right that she wraps up this chapter on her own.

'Do you think you'll be able to make it?' she asks Zach.

'Um, I might be working...'

'That's okay. I'll come in and see you again before I leave.'

He nods again.

'At least... you got to find out what happened,' he adds, his meaning obvious.

People seem keen to mention it to her, so clearly relieved to find some sort of justice at the end of the tale.

***

In the car park, Zoya reaches the minibus and unlocks the door. The first edges of shadow are forming at the base of the town hall.

She climbs up into the driver's seat and removes the bag from her shoulder, opening the glove compartment to leave the stack of flyers for Luke. Rummaging around to make space for them, she notices something that she has seen before – the thin strip with the hole and the wires. She puts it back, none the wiser, stows the flyers and sits back in her chair.

Her attention is drawn to the high reaches of the hill-tops beyond the river and the faint speckle of soaring birds, until the town hall clock chimes four and she knows it is time to get back.

***

Zoya pulls the bus through the leafy gates and admires the new, sharply painted sign that Toby is hammering into place. They have picked a really hard-to-miss spot. She parks up, facing the outdoor stage.

She lays her forearms on the wide steering wheel and slumps there, watching the busy scene.

At the site of the stage, many hands are making light work. Dancers and tutors and local kids are busy with paint brushes all over the structure. Reed is there among the painters and Luke is sweeping a section of the floor. Dan and Leon are discussing the metal rigging and the whole renovation seems to be coming together nicely.

Zoya looks around at the local kids, happy to stay and help after their classes; at the dancers, pulling their weight between rehearsals; at the simple hopefulness of the dance school willing to move on.

She should feel happier than this.

Not happy, exactly – none of it can undo the horrible events – but *something*. Everyone had expressed some kind of gratitude to her today: that Sharon's killer has been caught and charged with murder. Zoya should feel some measure of closure, like they do, but she doesn't. Something catches at her breath: an emptiness in the depths of her; a leaden, sinking darkness that won't go away.

She slumps further in her pose, her face almost hidden behind crossed arms. Inside, she is feeling that particular hollowness that you can only truly ache from on such a glorious day.

***

Over at the outdoor stage, Reed pauses, paintbrush in hand, and wipes his brow on his forearm. He can hear Dan and Leon talking as they work. So far today, they have covered quantum computing, medical dramas and the Eurovision Song Contest, as well as football, Tolkien and beer.

Reed notices the minibus parked up, ready to take the kids home. He peers beyond the reflective glass, trying to spot Zoya. Registering her body language, his expression droops to a concerned frown.

'Bus is here, kids!' Luke is calling out, holding out a tub to collect their paintbrushes. Then, to Reed, 'They don't seem to want to leave.'

Then he raises his voice again.

'Kids! Zoya's here to take you home!'

***

Zoya's bowed head jerks up at the sound of light tapping at the passenger door. She flicks the lever that opens it. A breath of grassy air flows into the bus and Toby is standing there.

She notices that he has tucked the hammer away in his tool belt and is leaning casually on one crutch, squinting and smiling up at her.

'How are you finding it?' he asks. 'The turning circle's not too bad, is it?'

'Oh, the minibus. Yeah, think I've got the hang of parking it now. How's the leg?'

'Almost healed,' he says, smiling again. 'It's not too much for you, all this ferrying kids around, is it?'

'Oh' – she shakes her head – 'no. I mean, I'm sharing it all with Luke anyway, so…'

'But thanks, though, Zoya – thanks for stepping in.'

Toby looks off toward the almost-finished outdoor stage.

'Going to be really something. Oh' – he sees the kids heading their way and flashes his eyebrows at her. 'Here they come!'

JUNE

CHAPTER 31

On the morning of the day before the performance, Zoya, Reed and Dan are sitting on the grass together, next to the van.

Reed picks at the lawn, finding a thick blade of grass satisfyingly succulent and squeaky between his fingers.

'Shouldn't you be busy rehearsing your piece?' Dan asks, curiously.

Zoya shakes her head.

'No, we're all doing an easy jazz class this morning, just for fun, and then I'm going to try to not...'

'Try to not...?' Reed echoes, an arch to his eyebrow.

She smiles.

'Try to not over-rehearse...'

'*Not* rehearse?' Dan queries gently.

Zoya shrugs happily.

'Well, if we don't know it by now...'

They look across the grounds. Everything seems to swell with colour in the growing sunshine. There is the newly renovated outdoor stage all ready for the show. The site seems oddly deserted – now that the army of renovators have gone.

'What are you planning to do next, Zoya? After this is all over?' Dan asks.

Zoya takes in a long breath.

'I don't know.'

Her voice matches Dan's in gentle curiosity, as if the answer will eventually drift her way, but not today.

A bee, momentarily confused by the windscreen, bats gently into the glass before bobbing around the vehicle and zig-zagging across the field, from bloom to sun-sweetened bloom.

'What about staying on at the dance school?' Dan continues. 'Isn't that administrator guy…?'

'Luke,' Reed adds, supplying his name.

'… leaving soon? Maybe you could run that new community programme they're starting up?'

'After you made them start it,' Reed jokes.

'I didn't *make* them, I…'

She catches Reed's eye and his teasing expression and punches him softly on the arm. He pretends to fall over and assumes a dramatic position, sprawled on the summery grass.

He stays down, watching a ladybird crawling along a dandelion stalk.

'What about joining our merry band of itinerant paranormal investigators?' Dan suggests, accompanied by a flash of his brows.

Reed rolls forward onto his elbows and picks a daisy from the lawn.

'Ummmm…' she says, drawing out the word in a hum.

Dan puts on his wide-brimmed fedora to protect his eyes from the strengthening sunshine.

'What about your dad, Zoya?' Reed asks her, looking up from his close communion with nature.

'Oh, Dad and Abigail are still in America. They sent me a good luck message, though.' She subconsciously touches the hip pocket of her dungarees. 'Talking of *messages*…' she says, sitting up straight and adopting a gossipy tone. She taps Reed on the shoulder, causing him to look up. 'Maybe it's *you* who's got a reason to stick around?'

Dan opens one eye to check which 'you' she is talking about. She seems to be looking at *him*.

'Somebody was talking to us about you, weren't they, Reed?'

Reed sits up from the grass to join in.

'Yep,' he nods, grinning.

Zoya nods.

'He's into you, Dan.'

Dan looks from one to the other, frowning with disbelief.

'Just "working on the rigging" together, eh?' Reed teases.

'Leon?' Dan says, incredulously. 'He's my engineering buddy, that's all.'

'Not from what he was saying to us,' Zoya counters.

'Seriously, man,' Reed adds. 'He was asking if you were single and everything.'

Dan shakes his head.

'No, no, no… I don't know why you're saying this. Leon's a… a…' – he stumbles over his sentence – 'like a perfect human, in, like, the most perfect shape that a guy can be…'

Zoya and Reed adopt matching expressions.

'What I'm saying is,' Dan continues, standing and picking up his washbag and towel, 'he would never be interested in a...'

Dan's protestations tail off as he sees the expressions on their faces. He gives up and starts walking toward the residential block.

'I'm serious, though, Dan!' Zoya calls after him. 'He did!'

***

Shortly after Dan goes off to get his shower and avoid their matchmaking chat, Zoya has to leave for her class.

After she leaves, Reed leans over to pick up her dad's postcard that has slipped out into the grass.

CHAPTER 32

'Aren't you coming back with us?' Sandy asks, one foot on the coach steps.

He has noticed Zoya hesitating in the car park.

She sees Toby fiddling with the glove compartment and looks away fast.

'Come on, last trip back on the fun-bus together?' Tilda says, poking her head out from inside the vehicle.

Zoya looks around the square.

'No, I'll make my own way back – it's okay, I'll see you back there for the dinner. I've... I've just got something else to do...'

She smiles, but knows it looks weak and unconvincing.

'I'm not having it,' Lauren says. 'You're *family*, man,' she insists.

Zoya's feet don't move.

'No, honestly, I'll see you back there in a bit. You all go without me.'

'We'll wait!' Sandy announces.

Tilda and Lauren both adopt a puzzled frown.

Zoya glances for a split second at the police station beyond the car park and then forces a confident, sunny smile.

'Go, go!' she insists in a cheery, upbeat tone. 'I'm not coming back yet.'

Soon enough, the coach is pulling out of the carpark and, as it curves away, Sandy, Tilda and Lauren are standing by the back seats, dancing around for Zoya's amusement. She stands stock still and waves at them as they leave, matching their hand jive gestures for a moment before waving goodbye.

After the coach disappears around the corner and out of sight, Zoya turns to face the police station again. She walks up to the entrance and goes straight in.

At the duty desk she explains herself.

'I want to report a crime.'

She feels inside her bag for the strip of plastic with the pinhole and takes a deep breath.

***

Later, she is sitting in the waiting area, staring glumly at the fading afternoon outside.

'Sorry, miss, as I explained…'

'It's *Ms*.'

'What?'

'It's *Ms*.'

'Oh, er, *Ms*… there's nobody to take your statement yet. Perhaps you'd prefer to come back tomorrow?'

'No,' Zoya says firmly. 'I'll wait.'

The duty sergeant pauses, looking at her, before getting on with his busy shift. Zoya sits back and looks out of the window once more. The town square is the same as ever but there is even less people-watching to be had than usual and Zoya is bored.

I'm not leaving, she thinks.

She has noticed that a couple of replacement floor tiles are the wrong colour and that the neighbourhood watch poster isn't on the wall quite straight. The rumblings of the traffic flowing around the square are irritatingly irregular. Sometimes she hears footsteps inside the station, just around the corner, but nobody appears. The plastic chair is pressing a jutting lip in the underside of her thigh.

She sees the parade of shops and the town hall and the old stone bank across the road. She recognises the person at the cashpoint outside it. *I know that backpack and that bike.*

That's Luke, she notices fondly, with a bittersweet smile. It's his last week at the dance school too, she gathers, as he's leaving for a new job, doing something she can't remember, somewhere else. She resolves to catch up with him at the leaving party tomorrow night and find out.

She thinks back to the first day, feeling lost in the lanes. She remembers driving through the gateway and seeing Luke with his sign. She thinks of the first-night welcome party – everyone wearing stickers with their names. She tries to excavate her first impressions of people who would later become friends, but it's impossible – she knows them all too well.

She thinks of the night visits, staying up talking in other people's rooms – the small hours, wrapped in blankets, when the short shuffle along the corridor seemed too far and they put off sloping back to their own beds. She remembers when they discovered the ping pong table and the time that she and Clare nearly got locked in Studio 5.

She remembers the breakfasts and the dash for extra coffee before the daily digest began. She can almost see the ever-changing noticeboard and that particular timetable font.

She knows the colour sequence of the striped coach seats by heart. She remembers the time she and Jo were laughing so much that they had to separate and sit in other seats.

How much time has she spent mooching around this small town on the Friday trips, how many shared scones, how many rounds in the pub?

She thinks about the Red Dragon Chinese restaurant: the curve of the seating, the way the waitress does her hair. She remembers how Lauren always ordered the same thing: chicken with black bean sauce.

She looks at the low stone wall in front of the police station and picks out the exact spot where she has sat, many times, waiting for the lift home.

She blinks and looks up again. Luke is still there at the cash point. His transaction seems to be taking forever. She focusses on his movements – repeatedly jabbing his fingers at the number pad; slipping his hand into and out of his backpack; lots of looking behind. *Furtive*, she thinks, the soft smile falling from her face. Unmistakeably *furtive*. As he turns again, she sees him folding a piece of paper and tucking it away in his pocket – and suddenly she *knows* that it must be a list of four-digit numbers and very familiar names.

All those Friday trips into Rithling, helping people get set up with bank accounts, advising Sharon what to do with all that cash… *such a helpful chap*.

She jumps up and sees him reaching for the mountain bike that he has leant against the wall. Then she dashes through the doors and across the tarmac.

Racing across the square, she sees that Luke has mounted his bike and is zipping away, along the road. What can *she* do on foot?

In an effort to try and spot him, she rushes to the vantage point on the path that crosses the riverside steps. At least, seeing the direction he takes would be something useful to report.

She stands on the high path where it bridges the alley, desperately looking one way, then another. Then she sees the bike begin a bobbing descent down the steps below. Luke is making his way down to the low road by the water – she can see his face quite clearly, and, as she stares, he also sees *her*.

'Luke Boyd!' she calls. '*You're* the thief!'

The accusation seems to shock him. Then he loses control of the bike.

She sees the dark mass of him and the tyres and frame and saddle; falling, tumbling now, down the steep, stone stairway in a gear-whirring, metal-bending, flesh-bruising dive. She can hear the crunching rattle of his bike crashing down the passageway, scratching pale streaks in the stone like wounds.

She rushes around to the alley, alarmed at the accident, and sees Luke, bike and backpack strewn on the steps below. The contents of his bag have spilled, and he is moving but not getting up.

At the bottom of the steps, two policemen have begun their climb. They are still clutching the takeaway coffees and sticky buns that they have bought from the café by the river but set the snacks down when they see the accident.

'That's evidence!' Zoya calls to them, beginning to jog down from the top step and pointing at Luke's bag of things. She sees it all in detail now, just as the policemen do – many bits of plastic that look a lot like cloned bank cards and wads and wads of cash, scattered all over the steps.

She fumbles in her bag and holds up the camera strip. It was never about spying on the dancers' bodies – just their fingers as they punched in numbers at the cashpoint. All those early bike rides, she realises – perfect for setting it up.

'He's been copying bank cards and stealing from us! And one of the victims was *Sharon Surtees.*'

The policemen both look grave at the mention of Sharon's name, and then move into slick, professional action, radioing the station and approaching the sprawled man with care. One of the officers starts collecting the scattered evidence from the steps, the other places a hand on Luke's shoulder – part comforting gesture, part strong arm of the law.

Zoya watches Luke for a long time, willing him to look at her again. He just sits sullenly on the step, clutching a painfully twisted knee. She doesn't take her eyes from him but all she can see is the top of his bowed head. When the policeman questions him, he just hangs his head lower and looks away.

Zoya shouts.

'She'd still be alive if it wasn't for *you*! You know that?! Sharon would still be *alive*!'

CHAPTER 33

On the afternoon of the Midsummer Show – their final performance – the weather is playing along: pleasant, not too breezy, clear sunny skies but not too hot. The newly renovated outdoor stage looks perfect. Everyone who has had any involvement with the project shares a quiet satisfaction to see it now – finished, cleaned up and filled with people looking forward to a show.

Zoya scans the rows, spotting the young dancers from their community programme who have brought family members along. It makes her smile to see the school all opened up like this and the faces of local people, not entirely sure what to expect. She locates Reed and Dan in the crowd, talking and reading through the programme. From a distance, they seem like an odd-couple double act, she thinks, watching them share face-crumpling laughter together. She smiles.

Up on the lawn in front of the dance school, she sees her fellow dancers warming up. She should think about joining them. Leon is there in his leg warmers, casually waiting for her and stretching out his hips and limbs. Now that they have moved the show outside, they have had to rethink their original idea about making him seem invisible with costume and lighting, but it's okay. The piece is something different now – a solo dance, with help.

People seem to think it works – the sections with Leon lifting her forming a sort of pulse in the choreography, each phase of the dance throwing the other into relief. Like music, Reed had said when she told him: verse, chorus, verse.

As she makes her way up the hill, Zoya sees the last pair arriving. Toby and Marianne, linking arms, and making their way to their seats.

Everyone is here now. The show can begin.

***

Zoya's feet pad-pad on the boards as Leon sets her down on the ground for the final time. The soft noise is quieter on her ear than the rustling branches of the trees at the distant perimeter, but she can still hear it; the gentle two-beat repeating in memory, like the endless waves of the sea.

After a moment's quiet, the audience begins applauding vibrantly. The wildness of their cheering has been growing with every performance and the apprehensive new audience members seem to be enjoying the show.

Zoya and Leon hold hands and take parallel bows. Gradually, Zoya returns from that place of imagining and starts to see faces in the crowd again.

Leon takes a large stride backwards and gestures for Zoya to take the credit, urging her with a flicker of his eyes to take the solo bow that she deserves. She obliges. A movement in the crowd draws her attention and she sees Reed almost up on his feet, aiming for a standing ovation but being swiftly pulled back down to his seat by Dan's hand on his shirt. Others wouldn't have noticed, but it makes her grin. She carries the feeling in a beaming smile as she scoots off the stage and jogs up the grassy rise. She sits on the ground with the other performers and receives compliments and pats on the back.

***

Dan faces Reed with an expression that is waiting for an audience, but Reed affects preoccupation; running his finger down the programme, concentrating on the listings, and trying his hardest not to notice Dan's comical stare.

Reed's finger moves down the printed programme as he reads the entry:

'There Is Another Sky'
Performed by Zoya Carmichael and Leon Foster
Choreography by Zoya Carmichael.

The next entry in the programme is for the final dance. He reads the title – *'The Never-Ending Fall'* – then looks up to see three dancers, all women, taking up their positions in a pattern on the stage. They leave an obvious, unoccupied gap. Zoya has already explained this; it is the place where Sharon should have danced.

The dancers take their time, standing in position, eyes cast downward, centring themselves. The audience hushes.

Reed watches the still line of dancers expectantly, think-ing, over and over again; *one in four, one in four...*

He hears himself catch a breath.

Up on the grassy bank, behind the seated rows, the dancers reach for hands and lay arms around shoulders. They settle into stillness and watch the stage with wide, moist eyes.

... five, six, seven, eight...

CHAPTER 34

I'm walking along the ravine path, high above the invisible river that snakes its way through the dark drop below.

I have just passed the point where Reed appeared that time but tonight I am alone.

I'm enjoying the shush of my steps along this path. It goes with the tune of the flowing river – tinkling, wayward splashes bubbling over the rocks. I see summer growth feathering the path-side and trees jewelled with berries that wink in the light.

I look around at the curling shadow of hills ranged beyond the river, greys warming to green, everything orange-washed, ready for the dawn. I look up and notice the night sky, pale and receding, sprinkled still with fading stars.

The breeze catches the very ends of my hair, balmy and gentle, like a caress. I'm walking toward the bridge. I still want to. Despite everything. Maybe, *because* of it.

The hills are brightening slightly, revealing themselves in the first glimmers of light from the waking sun. I often think we should come up with a new word for this time – the magical turning point after the night and before the dawn.

I walk on toward the bridge.

Someone has chalked something on the floor, so I stop to read it.

'Reasons why the world is a better place for having you in it'

I smile at the sentiment. What a lovely thing for someone to hear. Most people are not bad people, I remind myself. I need the reminder. Maybe *I* should chalk that down everywhere I go to keep on reminding myself. *Most people are good people.* And some are the best human you will meet.

I walk on, cheered by the random discovery. This is still a place undefined by what happened to Sharon here. This is still a road that takes people from home to friends and adventures. This is still a path that gives an amazing view of a beautiful valley – up ahead, where the dark river runs beneath the bridge.

Something else is on the path ahead of me: a chalk circle with something in it. I have a thought and look around but don't see him. I look back to the ground.

The chalk circle is enclosing the postcard from Dad and Abigail that I thought I had mislaid. I pick it up and turn it over a couple of times, the dawn light shining off the glossy picture of New York. I read their good luck message and see the margin of cramped kisses which makes me think of glittering stars. Reed must have found it somewhere. Why has he left it here for me to find?

I walk on. Another chalk circle and a magazine. I pick it up – *The Lowdown* – and see a biro message:

'Remember this? Thanks for keeping my spirits up when everything was going down. Karen xxx'

I look at the picture. There we are – dancing our hearts out and laughing together, snapped in an Edinburgh night-club. I do remember.

I place Dad's postcard in the page like a bookmark, fold the magazine closed and hold it to my chest. I take a breath and look along the path ahead of me. I think I know why he's doing this, but there isn't any need.

The trail continues along the pavement, drawing me on from circle to circle…

Next, a child's drawing of some stick figures in wobbly circles. A neat note has been added by a grown-up on the reverse:

'This is how Jack still thinks of you – he calls you the "lula loop lady"! Come visit for more hooping fun soon! Love from Issy and Jack xxx'

Then, an orienteering map with scribbles:

'We made it! When's the next adventure? Miss you, mate. Cal x'

A small box containing a tattered board game, the message from Jane written inside the lid.

'Remember our trip to the cottage? It would have been a total washout with a lesser companion. You don't think Mr Wellies would mind that I half-inched our new favourite weird old game, do you? Must get together again soon. Hurry up – it's your turn!'

I think about Cal, Jane, Issy and Jack. How did Reed get hold of these things? How did he know? Cally lives way up in Aberdeen – did he go all the way up there just for this?

I collect them all as I go – an armful of keepsakes.

I am on the bridge now, almost halfway. I see the owl figurine from Sharon that I found in our room. I've already got the note she wrote in my wallet. I have committed it to memory. I have hardly forgotten *her*.

I stand up again with my little pile. I am nearing the centre of the bridge. I peer at the path ahead of me – are there any more things he left for me to find? I approach another chalk circle.

It's my lost address book – which explains a few things. And there, on the cover, is that photograph of the three of us: Dad and Aunt Abigail and me. I get a strange shiver from looking at it – from looking at myself with that smile. I can't help thinking about those photographs of Sharon: the police one that nobody recognised her from, and my one – where she looks happy and laughing and free.

I doubt anyone has seen *me* with *that* smile in a long time.

I take my small collection of keepsakes and place them gently in a neatly tucked pile in the corner of a strut and the iron wall of the bridge. I rise and place my hands on the rail to watch the narrow valley catching the colours of daybreak.

It occurs to me that this weird treasure trail is Reed's way of stopping me – of giving me important things to carry back to the dance school; things that waking would separate from me; things that wouldn't survive the fall.

Before I get all caught up in resenting him for interfering, I remember what he wrote for me at the start: *Reasons why the world is a better place for having you in it* – a *really* lovely thing for someone to hear.

I smile. No, he means well. He just thinks some falls are too big to recover from – even in a dream. He's not being controlling; he just wants to cheer me up.

I hear his footsteps and smile.

When I turn, he is walking toward me quite tentatively from the other side of the river. He is carrying something which he holds out to me.

'Aren't you finishing your treasure trail?' he asks, gesturing in the direction he came from.

I see the soft scatter of the chalk circle scuffed by his feet.

He hands me an old flyer advertising open auditions for a play:

'My dear sweet Zoya, your encouragement to go to this audition changed my life. Who would have thought that my twilight years would be the most creative, most sociable and most fulfilling era I have known? It was because of this play that Frances saw me on stage and we were able to find one another – after all this time. Thank you, sweet child – your mother would have been so proud of the woman you have become. Yours, in loving gratitude, George.'

This one brings a lump to my throat. I lock eyes again with Reed.

'Thanks. Thanks for doing all this for me. Did you really go to Aberdeen?'

He looks unusually sheepish and nods. He is closer now, close enough for me to see his focus darting from one of my pupils to the other. He's trying to read my reaction and what I'm going to do next.

'Where did you materialise from anyway?' I ask.

'Oh, my van's parked around that rise.'

He must mean the spot where the road exits the ravine bridge and begins to climb a weaving route over the hills.

'Great. Could you look after my things in your van for me until tomorrow?'

I try not to say it any way that might come out sounding ungrateful, but his face falls anyway. I fill the silence with one of our in-jokes.

'If we move things, they stay moved?'

Reed glances out along the valley.

'Oh, okay. What are you going to do?'

I look out at the landscape. I don't want to ask him to leave. Because I don't want him to.

We see the dawn reflection simmering in the distance, seeds of scattered light sown past the pleated peaks and perches to decorate the long river like a twinkling path. Beneath us, the water swirls around the same rocky meanders, cresting white and cornering the same eddied route toward the distant sea.

'Hey, do you think Dan believed us?' I ask, and we both laugh a little, shake our heads and widen our eyes.

I love how easy it is for us to snap onto the same wavelength sometimes. I note his long, slim hands floating around his body as he enacts a dramatic shrug. It's always feels like being let into a secret when he transforms from the still, cool, observer, into the witty, silly, charismatic man he really is.

'I really do appreciate it, you know,' I say. '*Reasons why the world is a better place with me in it.*'

'Oh, I just… felt you needed cheering up' – he seems bashful again, his voice trailing away on the air – 'and, I, I mean, I wish *I* had people who felt…'

He uses his fingers to paint out the rest of the sentence. I catch his flailing hand and hold it. His skin is always warmer than it looks. He looks me in the eye as I squeeze his hand gently. The daylight falls softly over his face and his eyes transform from night grey to dawn green.

He knows what I mean.

I can see the flecks of gold in his irises now and the left-right dance of his gaze again. His hair slowly falls forward on his brow. I can smell the shampoo he uses. His skin is fresh and shaved and smooth.

'So, what now?' he asks eventually, looking down at me from not quite his full height.

I move away to the bridge rail again, letting his fingers slip from mine. I grasp the rail-top decisively, peering down to the drop below. Then I look back and up at him to reply.

'I'm jumping.'

He erupts in an exasperated sigh and spins away from me before checking himself, nodding a couple of times ever so slightly, and turning back, calm and measured once again.

'Sorry,' he says earnestly. 'You don't want me spoiling it for you – I'll go.'

'No! Don't go,' I answer quickly. 'You don't have to go.'

'Okay, but I can't watch,' he says, turning his back to me neatly like a gent in an old movie, looking away while a lady gets changed.

Using the struts and giant bolts as footholds, I climb up onto the broad, flat top of the metal wall. I sit there, gathering my breath. I can hear the run of the dark water rippling over the rocks.

I sit there a while longer. Nobody says anything.

I turn back to look at Reed. He is still standing, back turned, patiently waiting, but I can see his fingers agitating one another and his back rising and falling with quick, tense breaths. He glances at me over his shoulder, checking on the delay.

He walks up and starts the process of getting his own long legs onto the flat top of the bridge. I look at him with an open mouth.

'I'm jumping too,' he explains, mirroring my position, sitting on the wall, hands grasping the lip at the edge.

'You don't think it's dangerous anymore?' I ask.

He answers with a side-eyed glance before resuming his grave contemplation of the drop below.

'No,' I say, shaking my head. '*You* think it's dangerous. Don't. No, don't. I'm *not* asking you to do this.'

'I'm going to jump with you so that you can. I know how much you want to. It's okay, I'm here.'

I cock my head and narrow my eyes.

'If you think this is calling my bluff and will stop me doing it, it isn't. *I'm* jumping – *you* don't have to.'

'Okay, go ahead,' he says neutrally, then pulls his mouth into a small smile.

'I'm going to.' I sit there, nodding. 'Right. I'm jumping.'

I carefully rise to a stand. Out of the corner of my eye, I see Reed doing the same.

'What are you doing?'

'I told you,' he says, 'I'm jumping too. Are we doing a countdown?'

'Okay, but you're not holding my hand,' I instruct. 'Okay, but, just to check – you *are* doing this because you want to…?'

'No,' he says simply, 'I *don't* want to – I'm doing this for you.'

We are standing now, side by side, on the broad, flat ledge, above the deepest part of the ravine. The valley has fully caught the dawn now and its shadows are thawing with the daybreak.

I look at Reed again.

'This isn't going to get me to sleep with you, you know,' I say.

'I know.'

The daybreak is painting itself in watercolours across the sky.

'On your count,' he says. 'After… Zwiffle?'

We laugh.

'Why don't I count us in?' I suggest.

'Why *do* they start it there…?' he wonders.

'How do you mean?'

'Well, what happened to the one, two, three, four?'

We go quiet and look at the fall ahead of us, then look at one another and nod.

'Okay,' I announce, 'and five, six, seven, eight.'

We take off and my feet leave the solid metal of the bridge. And then the soft, caressing sky is all around us, catching us in the slow drift of time.

I fly; soaring lightness; a moment of impossible suspension. And then I feel like I'm falling but I never hit the ground…

***

Zoya, Reed and Dan are sitting at a terrace table outside the Second Breakfast Café, by the low road through the Rith Valley. The high span of the ravine bridge is way in the distance but Zoya can still make it out, her focus pulling back to it again and again. Reed's camper van is parked up across the road, gleaming in the sunlight, pointing in the direction of the distant coast.

'A hidden camera – I should have known,' Dan says wistfully.

'But you weren't here… you didn't know anything about it…' Zoya queries.

'No – the vanishing necklace,' Dan explains.

'I'd forgotten all about that!' Reed says.

'*I* hadn't.'

The overly grim way that Dan says it makes them all laugh.

A waiter approaches and sets down a tray of hot drinks on the picnic table: one tea, one black coffee, one cappuccino.

'Thanks,' Zoya says, as he picks up the emptied tray and heads back inside. She is wearing the purple *Liberte!* T-shirt that Leon gave her.

The friends set about gathering their drinks, creating a trio of small, coincidental splashes by adding rocks of sugar all at the same time.

They laugh again together. Then Reed begins stirring his drink and Dan takes to blowing over the top of his tea. Zoya cradles her mug while scanning the high crevices of the towering hills for birds on the wing.

She considers the looming hill face, softly cracked and scattered with sheltered perches – impossible crevices where no human has ever trod. Small trees poke their way out of sunny rock to grow horizontally, their leaves fluttering in the high breezes if you can spot them – if you stop and look.

Before long, Dan pauses his tea-cooling and sets the mug down on the wooden table.

'I...'

He looks up at them bashfully, from beneath the brim of his hat.

'I...'

He has their rapt attention. They watch his expression – serious and happy at the same time.

Dan exhales with resolve.

'I'm going to give it another go with Robin,' he says with a flickering little smile, then resumes his blowing over the hot tea.

Reed smiles softly. This is what he wanted for him all along. Zoya touches Dan's arm supportively.

The three friends enjoy their drinks and the quiet scenery and the day rolls on.

Dan begins to notice Reed and Zoya looking at one another, conducting some secret conversation with their eyes. Then they sit there across from him, looking as if this time *they* have something to say.

Dan looks from one to the other.

'What?'

Zoya and Reed's eyes flicker to one another and then back to Dan.

'Want to tell me why you two are acting oddly?' he asks, resting his big hands on the table, palms inquisitively to the sky.

Zoya looks at Reed again. His pose becomes a touch more awkward but there is assent to the dip of his head. She smiles at Dan.

'We've got something to tell you.'

Dan looks from her to Reed, who is now avoiding his eye, and back to Zoya again.

'You're getting married?' Dan asks, unable to interpret their mixed messages.

Reed is tracing a knot in the wood grain with a finger, but Zoya is looking Dan deep in the eye.

'No,' Zoya replies, with a slight shake of her head.

Reed raises an eyebrow a couple of millimetres and keeps watching his hand.

'You're having a baby?' Dan ventures, not entirely joking.

'No!' Reed says, looking up with a shake of his head and an amused lopsided grin.

Dan matches his quirky smile and then wets his lips, ready to try again.

'You two *are* telepathic!' Dan jokes, leaning forward.

Zoya giggles.

'No,' she counters calmly, then looks to Reed for final confirmation that she can say what she is about to say.

Reed screws up his eyes tightly and gives Zoya the tiny nod she is watching for.

'Are you sure?' she checks.

'What's the big secret?' Dan asks, prompting them to speed things up.

Reed opens his eyes and mirrors Dan's pose, forearms resting on the table.

'Okay.' He clasps his hands and takes a breath. 'Dan – serious question: Would you want to know something – even if it shakes your entire understanding of the world?'

Dan observes Reed's eyes trained on him, deep-set and sparkling like the river flowing by. He can tell that his friend is serious but not sombre. He gives the perplexing question some thought.

Zoya watches them and takes a sip of her drink. It's a good sign that Dan is properly considering the question. She watches him blinking as he thinks. Under the table, Reed finds Zoya's hand to grasp. She squeezes back.

The three friends remain so still and peaceful that a small sparrow lands on the picnic table between them, cocking its head this way and that, before flitting to the ground to prospect for food between their feet.

A soft breeze lifts a delicate strand of Zoya's hair, making it dance above her head.

Finally, Dan sits back in his seat and focusses on them. He takes off his fedora and sets it gently on the picnic table. He swallows and begins to answer.

'Well…,' he says thoughtfully, determined yet bright, moving his feet to match his new upright position; ready to deliver his verdict.

Fleeing the heavy boot, the sparrow flies, first to a bush by Reed's van at the roadside, and then to the low slate roof of the café. It hops along, jerking its head and scanning the terrace; the wooden tables; the intently talking friends; the gently spinning weathervane.

A moment later, the bird succumbs to wanderlust and takes off with fluttering wings. Higher and higher above the building and the rushing water, beyond the flash of sunlight glinting from the roof of the camper van; rising higher above the hillside, the stone walls of Rithling shrinking like a map; up, up to the thermals and the hilltops; away and away; lost and free in the gauzy distance of the sky.

THE END

If you enjoyed this book, please leave a review.
You will help other readers to find books they love and make the author very happy.

Follow Jenny Cutts on Goodreads, Bookbub and Patreon.
www.jennycutts.com

Titles in this series
The Invisible Body
The Long Lost Sunset
The Never Ending Fall

The Invisible Body

A strange ability. A discovered corpse. But will his supernatural sleuthing skills lead him into a killer's trap?

England, 1990. Reed has travelled his whole life in search of someone who understands him. So he's thrilled when his journey brings him to free-spirited Zoya, who shares his rare ability to dream-walk. But after his gift leads him to a hidden corpse, he becomes the prime suspect in the murder.

Despite the setback, Reed resolves to use his power to help crack the case.

When the real perpetrator delivers a violent threat, he's tempted to give up, slip into his camper van and hit the road again. After all, who would miss him?

Will Reed flee the tiny seaside town and abandon his new friends – or will he risk everything to expose the murderer?

The Long Lost Sunset

A haunted hotel. A mysterious plot. But who is running out of time?

Scotland, 1991. Dan is too busy working to have a relationship. So, when a paranormal investigation takes him to Edinburgh, at least he can catch up with old friends. But when he overhears a mysterious plot, he discovers another reason to stay.

Dan enlists the help of a friend with strange abilities but doesn't like what he finds. Soon, the hotel fills with secrets and he doesn't know who to trust.

When a ticking clock points to danger, Dan must decide whether to leave the only person he has ever loved.

Is it a matter of time before Dan's heart is broken or is the situation deadlier than that?

www.ingramcontent.com/pod-product-compliance
Lightning Source LLC
Chambersburg PA
CBHW030808200726

48285CB00015B/1589